Royal Sarala Weddings

Can these royal siblings find their perfect match?

Prince Rohan of Sarala has always known of the responsibility he was born into—destined to one day be king, but it hasn't stopped him from being a little rebellious! While his older sister, Princess Marisa, has always been accepting of her kingdom's long-standing traditions, it doesn't mean she agrees with them! But now it's time for them to step up and marry... Is it possible to tame the Sarala siblings?

Don't miss these fabulous books
from Nina Milne!

His Princess on Paper

When Prince Rohan meets his suitably arranged fiancée, Elora, from a neighboring island, he's shocked by the very undeniable and mutual chemistry he was *not* expecting! Maybe a convenient engagement can also be fun...?

Bound by Their Royal Baby

Princess Marisa of Sarala was never meant to take the throne. But when she discovers her one night with a perfectly delectable stranger has resulted in a pregnancy, suddenly *everything* in her life is about to change...forever!

Both available now!

Dear Reader,

When I started Marisa and Kieran's story, I had a plan for them...with a beginning point and an end point. All I can say is that they had other plans; they resisted their happy ending and there was a point when even I wondered if they would actually allow love and trust into their lives. So the plan didn't go exactly according to plan, but I hope you enjoy reading their story.

Nina x

BOUND BY THEIR ROYAL BABY

NINA MILNE

Harlequin

ROMANCE

 **Harlequin®**
ROMANCE

ISBN-13: 978-1-335-21602-1

Bound by Their Royal Baby

Copyright © 2024 by Nina Milne

 Harlequin Enterprises ULC
22 Adelaide St. West, 41st Floor
Toronto, Ontario M5H 4E3, Canada
www.Harlequin.com

Printed in U.S.A.

Nina Milne has always dreamed of writing for Harlequin Romance—ever since she played libraries with her mother's stacks of Harlequin romances as a child. On her way to this dream, Nina acquired an English degree, a hero of her own, three gorgeous children and—somehow!—an accountancy qualification. She lives in Brighton and has filled her house with stacks of books—her very own *real* library.

Books by Nina Milne

Harlequin Romance

Royal Sarala Weddings

His Princess on Paper

The Casseveti Inheritance

Italian Escape with the CEO
Whisked Away by the Italian Tycoon
The Secret Casseveti Baby

The Christmas Pact

Snowbound Reunion in Japan

Second Chance in Sri Lanka
Falling for His Stand-In Fiancée
Consequence of Their Dubai Night
Wedding Planner's Deal with the CEO

Visit the Author Profile page
at Harlequin.com for more titles.

To all the amazing people at Hampshire Hospitals, with a special thank you to the staff at the DTC. Your kindness and caring were phenomenal.

Praise for
Nina Milne

"*Their Christmas Royal Wedding* is an escapist, enjoyable and emotional contemporary tale that will touch readers' hearts with its beguiling blend of searing intensity, heart-warming drama and uplifting romance. Nina Milne writes with plenty of warmth and heart and she has penned a poignant and spellbinding romantic read."

—*Goodreads*

PROLOGUE

PRINCESS MARISA OF SARALA looked across at her friend and shook her head emphatically. 'Absolutely not. No way. Not happening.'

'Just hear me out,' Caro said, her green eyes sparkling as she topped up their glasses with the cocktail that she had assured Marisa was 'mostly juice'. Though to be on the safe side Marisa was drinking the bright orange concoction slowly, appreciating each sip that mixed the sweetness of passion fruit with the tart taste of lime and a definite kick of something.

Marisa sighed. 'OK. I'll listen but I am not doing it. I am not joining a dating app.' That was a given.

'So, these are the facts,' Caro said. 'Fact number one. Your life is about to completely change. Correct?'

'Correct.' But it was a change she wanted with all her heart, though truth to tell she was still in shock at recent events. Just weeks ago, her younger brother, Rohan, had taken an un-precedented step in Saralan history and tra-dition and decided to abdicate his position as heir to Sarala, a small but prosperous Indian island that had been ruled by the royal Kamo-dian dynasty for centuries, passing from male ruler to male heir.

'Fact number two. Right now on Sarala legal bigwigs are racing around working out how to upend tradition, drag Sarala into the twenty-first century and allow a female to become heir to the throne. Said female being you.'

'Also correct.' Marisa sensed most of them weren't happy about it—come to that, her parents weren't exactly happy about it either. Her whole life her parents had wanted her to be someone different from who she was and that had made their relationship complicated enough throughout her childhood. But then ev-erything had been made worse when Marisa had messed up big time.

Even now remembered humiliation shud-dered through her, along with a jolt of regret, a wish she could go back in time and change her own reckless actions. But she couldn't and those actions had cost her so much: she'd lost her par-ents' respect and she had spent the last ten years trying to regain it. But she wasn't sure she'd succeeded, sensed their doubts as to whether she was capable of, *worthy* of, being heir.

Worry touched her, anxiety at the question she barely dared voice. What if they were right? What if she couldn't do this? Wasn't up to the job? Marisa knew her parents loved her, but she knew too that they loved Sarala more. Past events had proved that. If she messed up again, she'd be out. Again. Exiled. Again.

Enough—the past needed to be left in the past.

The most important thing now was that her parents had agreed to give her a chance and she would prove to them that she could do this. Could be heir and could eventually rule the kingdom as a good, just, fair ruler. Could take Sarala forward, make it a prosperous, happy place.

Caro waved a hand in front of her face. 'Earth to Marisa! Can I continue?' Without waiting for an answer, she did exactly that. 'While legal matters are being attended to, you have come to stay in London, staying out of the limelight, and now you're having dinner with me, one of your oldest friends and ex-sister-in-law, during this, your last week of freedom.'

'Corr—' Marisa broke off. 'No! That's not how I see it at all.' Though trust Caro to be dramatic; she was after all a renowned actress, with a string of prestigious awards behind her. Which was why Marisa had insisted on having dinner in Caro's house and had made sure she'd slipped in unobserved.

'The opposite, in fact. I want this, Caro. My whole life I have felt how unfair it was that, despite being older, I couldn't be heir to Sarala. Maybe I wouldn't have minded if Rohan had really wanted the job, but he didn't. You know that.' Or maybe Caro didn't. Despite having once been married to Rohan, a marriage that had been utterly disastrous, Caro had never really understood Rohan. 'I want this. For me, this *is* freedom.'

Caro shrugged. 'Fine. Wrong choice of words. I meant this is the last week where you can fly under the radar, do something as plain old Princess Marisa, sister to the heir of Sarala. It's your last chance to actually go on a real date without public scrutiny.'

'There's no way I am going on a dating app as myself; the people of Sarala would not be impressed with their princess being on a dating app.'

'OK. We'll set your profile up as a "normal", non-royal person. Your date need never know you are a princess. Come on, Marisa, it'll be fun. Something to store in your memory bank. What can possibly be wrong with that?'

Marisa opened her mouth to point out all the answers and then paused to truly consider the question. Did Caro have a point? Her life was about to change in ways she could barely fathom, and she would never be able to fly under the radar again.

Aware that she'd been silent a while, she looked up to see Caro grinning at her. 'Look. I've already set you up with a profile.'

'Caro...' But her protest sounded half-hearted even to herself. She sighed. 'Fine.'

'Perfect.' Caro beamed at her. 'I'll take it from here.'

*The same evening,
elsewhere in London*

Kieran Hamilton looked across at his friend and business partner, and shook his head emphatically. 'No. Absolutely not. No way. No. End of discussion.'

'It wasn't exactly a discussion,' Mark pointed out. 'I made a suggestion and—'

'I said no. So there is no need for a discussion.'

'Because you're worried I have a point?'

'No. Because I don't want to waste your time.' Kieran tried a smile. 'Mark, I appreciate you mean well, but I have absolutely no wish to go on a date, so there is no point in me joining a dating app.'

'Not now or not ever?' Mark asked.

It was a fair question, albeit not one Kieran wanted to think about. 'I'd be a fool to say not ever, but I can't imagine ever having a relationship again.' Not after the death of his wife. Aisla. Memories threatened to overwhelm him. Loss. Pain. Grief. Four years on and there was still the same searing, rending pain of guilt. Kieran wouldn't, couldn't try to replace Aisla; he owed her and their unborn child more than that.

'I get that,' Mark said, his voice gentle. 'But I'm not proposing a relationship. I'm suggesting a date. One evening, a small taste of life, a strings-free dinner in a nice restaurant with a woman. Then you can get back to your reclusive hermit-style life in the depths of Scotland. What harm can one dinner do?'

'I like my reclusive life.' Belatedly he unfolded his arms, reminded himself there was no need to be defensive. There was nothing wrong with his life. He'd bought a house that needed a massive amount of renovation in the middle of nowhere and that was how he'd spent the past eighteen months. Ever since the company he and Mark and Lucy had started had taken off, when he had felt he could leave without letting them down. Once he'd left, he'd needed something, a project that exhausted him physically so he could at least sleep some nights, without the recurrent nightmares. It was only at Mark and his wife Lucy's insistence that he visited London at all.

'I get that too. All I'm suggesting is that you put yourself out there for one night. It won't mean anything. You can be abundantly clear when you arrange it that it's just a dinner. Hell. You might not even get any hits.'

'Ha-ha-ha!' This from Lucy as she walked in holding three beers. 'You'll get plenty of hits.' Her expression became serious. 'Do it to make Mark happy. Make us happy.'

Kieran sighed, glanced at Mark and realised that Lucy had a point. He knew they worried about him. They'd all been friends for years, since meeting at university. So, he conjured up a smile, a rueful shrug of his shoulders.

'Fine. I'll do it.'

Lucy clapped her hands. 'Great. Now leave it to us.'

CHAPTER ONE

*Three days later,
still in London*

MARISA, OR RATHER MARINA, the name she was assuming for the duration of this date, a date she still couldn't believe she'd agreed to, walked along the crowded pavement from the Tube station, her steps slow as she enjoyed the light evening breeze, the feeling of anonymity as she mingled with people hurrying from work or to meet friends, all utterly oblivious to her royal presence.

Glancing at her watch, she realised she was running a little late and she increased her stride as she approached the restaurant, a high-street pizza chain, and headed into the revolving door, so focused that she miscalculated and entered at the same moment as a man who was also in a hurry.

As they collided he reached out a hand to

steady her and for a fleeting second she could swear she felt something, a frisson of awareness, and she looked up at him. 'Sor—' she began and broke off as she looked up and into a pair of eyes so blue that she blinked. Blue eyes, blond hair, strong jaw. 'Sorry,' she managed, and hurriedly looked away, reached out to push at the door, which…wouldn't budge. 'I think it's stuck.'

'Let me try.'

He reached out and now she was mesmerised by the lithe, muscular swell of his forearm, the size and strength of his hand as it pushed against the bar. And suddenly the space seemed to shrink and all she was aware of was his sheer physical presence, a sense of solid muscular bulk, a fresh clean smell with a hint of… black pepper? Citrus? Lime?

Oh, goodness, what was she doing? Smelling the man? She closed her eyes, tried to ground herself, tried to figure out what was going on.

'Help is on the way,' he said, and she opened her eyes, swore she'd heard a hint of relief in his voice, looked up at him again and saw something flash in those intense blue eyes. There was that little shiver over her skin. Again.

Turning she saw a staff member fiddle with the door mechanism and then, thank goodness, as they both pushed the door glided round and they emerged into the busy bustle of the restaurant.

Now she turned to face the man, saw him properly for the first time. A shade over six foot, his hair a dark blond and cut very short. She hadn't imagined the blue of his eyes—sky blue and bright. Firm jaw and mouth and she figured this was a man who either worked out or had a physical job, the latter indicated by a quick glance at his hands and the burn of memory at his brief touch when they'd collided.

A dark blue shirt, sleeves rolled up against tanned skin, a jacket slung over one arm and he was holding a book. It took a second for the significance to dawn. Holding a book—that was how she was supposed to recognise her date. Which meant...

'Are you Kieran?'

'Yes.' His gaze was still focused on her, his blue eyes unreadable. 'You must be Marina.'

She opened her mouth to correct him, remembered just in time that Kieran knew her as Marina Carmody and that was the way it was going to stay. 'Yes,' she said instead.

There was a moment of silence and now those blue eyes definitely held something, a flash of what looked to Marisa like surprise, but not in a good way judging by the sudden tightening of his lips, the clench of his jawline.

Great. Presumably she didn't measure up to expectations. Perfect. Her long-dormant hormones, schooled to remain in sleep mode, had suddenly decided to wake up and party for a man who looked distinctly unimpressed to see her. Marisa narrowed her eyes.

Kieran might be drop-dead gorgeous but good looks meant nothing. Never judge a book by its cover, handsome is as handsome does… Marisa knew all the cliches and she knew they were born of truth.

Her own past mistakes had taught her that, or at least her 'Past Mistake'. Memories she'd long since buried resurfaced and she could almost see Lakshan's face, handsome, laughing, the sparkling hazel eyes. He'd used his looks to lure her in, used the tug of attraction to make her dance to a tune of his calling. And she'd complied, believed in him; blinded by her hormones, smitten and charmed by the turn of his lips, the warmth in his eyes. Never again. That she'd vowed and it wasn't a vow she was about to break any time soon.

'Yes,' she repeated. 'That's me.' Her voice was taut and she hoped he'd grasped the 'take it or leave it' tone. After all, he must have seen her photo and she didn't look any different from that.

Curly black hair that she'd given up on straightening years ago, though tonight Caro had helped to tame the curls to fall in smooth waves to just past her shoulders. Her make-up was minimal, her large brown eyes with their sweep of dark lashes slightly enhanced, her lips glossy. But there was nothing she could do about her nose, which was frequently described as aquiline, or her mouth, which erred on the side of generosity. But she didn't look so bad, so he didn't need to look so dismayed. In fact, 'Is there a problem?' she asked.

He blinked, gave his head a small shake and then he smiled, a smile that held rue and even a hint of apology. 'No problem at all,' he said. 'On my side anyway. Any problem for you?' The smile widened slightly and she realised she was now standing in classic confrontational mode, arms folded, chin jutting out.

'No,' she said. 'All good here.' It wasn't as though she could turn and walk out based on a flash of emotion she wasn't even sure she'd read correctly.

'Then let's get to our table.'

They followed a waitress to a corner wooden table and once they were seated Marisa focused on every detail: the gloss of the pine, the tea-light candle in a flower-shaped candle holder, the small but elegant glass vase that contained a single white flower. Somehow concentrating on the detail grounded her, kept her attention from Kieran until she was sure her hormones were back under rigid control.

'I think it's a carnation,' he said and she'd swear his voice held amusement. 'And if you look at the wall to your left there is a very colourful print of a scene that I assume is set in Italy. And then if you turn your head, across the restaurant is a very large clock with Roman numerals on it. In case you are bored of looking at the table.'

Marisa looked up; his blue eyes were surveying her and to her disconcertment there was a smile hovering on his lips. And there it was again, a little flip in her tummy and now the warning bell rang loud and clear in her head. Feelings like this had once precipitated near disaster for her, had had a life-changing impact, warped her relationship with her parents and her country. And it had all started like this. The 'accidental' meeting with Lakshan, a smiling apology, a pair of amused brown eyes.

She took a deep breath. That was years ago; she was different then, a naïve eighteen-year-old. Now she was in control, would not let this spook or scare her. She was about to become heir to a kingdom; of course, she could manage a simple dinner with a man she'd never see again. So what if he made her tummy flip?

He was a very good-looking man. Caro would tell her to enjoy the flips, eat her pizza and get on with it.

Attraction happened. It didn't *have* to lead to disaster.

So she smiled, kept her expression deadpan, and said, 'I think clocks are a fascinating topic and perfect to discuss on a date. For example, did you know that the first grandfather clock was invented in the 1670s, that a grandmother clock is around twenty-five centimetres smaller than a grandfather one and...' She hesitated, searched her memory banks for any other information about clocks and drew a blank. Well never mind; she could bluff with the best of them. 'There is even such a thing as a Great Aunt Clock. As well as of course the Ancestor clock invented by Professor Jentime.' She stopped, met his gaze blandly.

He nodded. 'You're right. That is fascinating. Grandfather clocks are pendulum clocks and there are of course so many types of clocks, atomic, water, and many others, including of course the cuckoo clock, another immensely interesting type of clock, invented by Franz Anton Ketterer...' he paused a beat, and she was nearly sure his lips gave the smallest upturn, 'and then of course there is the less popular duck clock.'

'Duck clock?' For the briefest of instants she almost believed him. Almost. But as his blue eyes met hers in apparent wide eyed innocence her own eyes narrowed. 'Really?'

'Absolutely. Just as genuine as a Great Aunt Clock. You see how lucky it is? We definitely have a clock fascination in common. In fact, I could keep going all night.'

His voice was deep, the smile in his voice seemed to run over her skin and before she could stop herself, she heard her voice ask, 'Is that a promise?'

There was a pause and their gazes met and she saw the smile leave his eyes, and the blue cloud with shadows, and she could read something in his eyes that went deeper than the earlier dismay. Now he looked angry, almost disgusted. She had no idea where her flirty comment had come from—perhaps from a Marisa she'd long since banished. But she'd definitely got it wrong. This was a one-way attraction; that seemed clear from the look of near repulsion in his blue eyes, followed by an instinctive push-back of his chair as if he was preparing to leave.

Now mortification set in and she could feel colour heat her cheeks. Embarrassment and a shot of vitalising anger. Yes, she'd miscalculated, but this was meant to be a date, for Pete's sake; why bother going on a date if you weren't expecting a little bit of banter and flirtation? Which he'd started anyway.

But right or wrong wasn't the point; bottom line was this was a one-way attraction and Kieran was about to walk out. Marisa clenched her hands into fists. No way was he leaving first. She rose to her feet. 'This was clearly a mistake. Luckily, we haven't got as far as ordering. If you decide to stay enjoy your pizza.'

It took Kieran a second for the penny to drop, to compute the reason behind Marina's evident anger. Clearly his expression must have shown something of what he was feeling and she thought it was directed at her. When all the anger and repugnance had been directed at himself.

Because ever since he'd bumped into this woman in that revolving door he'd been poleaxed by the visceral jolt of raw desire that had hit him. And continued to pelt him with a welter of sparks so all he'd been able to think about was how it might feel to kiss her.

With the result that for a few heady minutes he'd smiled, flirted, and he'd felt…alive.

Which had slammed him with a sucker punch of guilt. Because he *was* alive and Aisla was dead, his unborn child had never even had a chance of life. And a few years later here he was, sitting opposite a beautiful woman, feeling 'heady and alive'. The idea caused a twist of self-disgust.

But that wasn't Marina's fault, and there wasn't only anger on her face. He'd seen a swiftly concealed look of mortification. And now she was about to walk out.

Swiftly he rose to his feet, stretched a hand out. 'Wait!' he said, thought for a moment she'd ignore him. 'Please,' he added. 'I can explain.'

She shook her head. 'No need. You don't need to explain. I misread the situation. Let's leave it at that. I'm out of here.'

'You didn't misread the situation.' Her eyes narrowed as she studied him. 'Can we sit down?'

Another hesitation and then she glanced around, as if aware that they were attracting attention. 'Fine.' She sat, perched on the edge of her seat, back ramrod straight. 'But the situation seems crystal clear to me. I *found*—' and he noted the heavy emphasis on the past tense '—you attractive. I *thought* it was mutual. Your expression made it abundantly clear I got that last bit wrong. End of.'

'No.' Kieran shook his head. 'I did, I *do* find you attractive.' He forced himself to hold her gaze, knew he owed her that truth. 'Very attractive. That's the problem. I wasn't expecting it.'

'What were you expecting? This is a *date*. I'm assuming you aren't just here for the pizza, given you could dial out for a takeaway pepperoni deluxe.'

'I don't know what I was expecting. I haven't dated for a while. My friends think I should get out more. I disagree, but I know they worry so when they suggested I try this I agreed.'

'So, you agreed to a date to make them happy?'

'Yes.'

'After that you didn't give a thought to the fact there would be a real person sitting opposite you?'

'No.' There seemed little point in denying it. 'Then I met you. I found you very attractive and I panicked.' Which sounded ridiculous, he knew.

'Why?'

A fair question, but he wouldn't, couldn't, tell her about Aisla.

'Because I'm not looking for a relationship of any sort. I was going to eat my pizza, be polite and be on my way.'

'Polite? How do you think that's going?'

The words tart, a scowl on her face, and he moved his hand in a so-so gesture. 'Could be better.'

'You think?' She studied his face. 'Look. I

sort of get where you are coming from. Truly. A friend persuaded me to do this as well, and for the record I definitely don't want a relationship either. The deal was always one date. That's not negotiable.'

His turn to ask, 'Why?'

She hesitated and he sensed she was choosing her words carefully. 'Like you, I haven't dated for a while. But now my life is about to change. I'm about to start a new job; one I've always wanted, running the family business. In India. I know it is going to take up all my time and commitment over the next few years. So, my friend suggested the date idea as a last opportunity to cut loose and have some fun for a while. So here I am. Or at least here I was. Thank you for the explanation, but I guess it's time to call it a night and free the table up for someone else.'

She rose again, held out a hand and, on automatic pilot, he stood, took her hand in his.

There it was again, a zing, an awareness, and she felt it too—he knew she did. A reaction that was completely illogical, completely over the top, but it existed. He could see the realisation in the widening of her eyes, the small intake of breath. The feel of her fingers against his palm, the cool sensation somehow turning an everyday gesture into something more, something intimate, a connection. And he was aware of a mad desire to tug her forward, around the angle of the table and kiss her. Now his eyes snagged on her lips, a mouth that looked made for kissing, and then he dragged his gaze back up to her eyes, eyes that held shock and sparked with desire.

Thoughts raced from synapse to synapse at lightning speed, leading to a decision before he was even aware of it. Because right here and now he wanted to give her what she'd signed up for. A real date before she left for a different continent. One night, too, where he could live in the moment. Not in the past. Secure in the knowledge that it was only for a short burst of time.

'I have a better idea,' he said. 'How about we start this date again?'

CHAPTER TWO

MARISA STARED AT HIM, her head reeling, as her gaze dropped to their clasped hands. Perhaps it was the knowledge that this attraction was mutual that was messing with her head. causing her to feel a bit fuzzy round the edges, governed by hormones instead of common sense. Perhaps it was the feel of his hand around hers, such a simple touch evoking a fizz of reaction, a sense that Kieran, for whatever reason, had come to a decision that was significant, a knowledge that she had caused it, that this attraction was taking on a life of its very own. Making her feel carefree, reckless, and her whole being revelled in that realisation.

Because this time it was safe. Finite. Risk free. Whatever the night brought there could be no entanglement, no danger in this. He wanted only today, she wanted only today. In that instant her decision was made. Tonight, she was Marina Carmody, and she was going to go for it.

'Hi. I'm Marina. You must be Kieran. Good to meet you.'

'Nice to meet you too.' Now he smiled, a genuine corker of a smile that held warmth and promise, the type of promise that made her dizzy, tempted her to forgo pizza, and suggest...

Suggest what exactly, Marisa?

Time to slow down and leash her hormones. To at least get to know this man a little better, a man who hadn't dated for a while, a man who she actually knew nothing about. Yet it was with palpable reluctance that she let go of his hand and she sensed an equal unwillingness on his part to relinquish hers.

As they sat down again, a waiter hurried up. 'I am so sorry to have been so long. I was asked to help out with setting up the band. It's our jazz night tonight. Hopefully you like jazz?'

'Love it,' Marisa said.

'While you're choosing what to eat, would you like a drink? We've got a special jazz cocktail.'

'Sounds perfect.'

'Same for me,' Kieran said.

Once the waiter departed, Marisa looked down at the menu. 'Not that there's much point me looking. I always have the same. Chillies, capers and olives.'

'Spinach, egg and Parma ham. That's my go-to pizza.'

'So, we both always stick to tried and tested.' Marisa frowned. 'Do you think that means something?'

'That people who choose the same pizza toppings are risk averse?' he asked. 'I don't know. Are you risk averse?'

Was she? She remembered the last time she'd taken a risk. And how foolish that had been. 'There are consequences to risk,' she said.

'Yes,' he said. 'There are. But sometimes, no matter how careful you are, things happen.'

There was a sudden shadow in his eyes and Marisa felt an urge to take it away. Whatever his reasons for not wanting a relationship, whatever baggage Kieran carried, for one night, surely, he deserved to put it down?

'In which case, perhaps we should have a rule for tonight, to be carefree rather than careful and maybe we should take a risk or two.'

He looked at her and as she met his gaze steadily, she felt something shimmer in the air, a connection, a sense that this moment was important. 'I like the sound of that.'

His voice was low and deep, felt like a caress, sent a shiver over her skin and she tried to keep her voice matter-of-fact as she looked down at the menu, not ready to let him see her response in her eyes. 'As a start I am going to add an extra ingredient to my pizza, try something I have never tried before. Jackfruit. I'll try that.'

'I'll up the stakes. I'll replace the ham and eggs with artichokes and feta.'

There was a smile in his voice but when she looked up, she sensed a challenge and a question as well. How far was she prepared to go? How much risk would she take and how many new things would she try? Did anything go?

Enough. Right now, this was about pizza toppings.

'I'll even up and replace my capers with aubergine and I'll add some truffle oil.'

Before he could respond the waiter returned with their cocktails. 'Before we end up with all the toppings, let's call it there.'

'Agreed.'

Once they had ordered she sipped her drink. 'That is amazing.' She pulled the menu towards her and scanned it, glanced up at him, wondering if it was some sort of sign. 'It's called a Hanky-Panky.' She sensed her voice tremble with laughter, saw him blink and then his answering smile. She couldn't help the laugh that bubbled up and then he chuckled and they were both laughing.

When they stopped chuckling she continued reading. 'It was invented by the very first female head bartender at the Savoy in 1903. She was called Ada Coleman and she made cocktails for royalty and for Mark Twain.' Definitely a sign—Ada Coleman was a female pioneer and that was exactly what Marisa planned to be. And somehow it felt as though she had Ada's blessing for however the evening panned out.

'To Ada,' he said. 'And to hanky-panky.'

They clinked glasses and she took another sip, relished the taste even more now she knew the origins of the cocktail. The sweetness of the vermouth was complemented by the sharpness of the gin, the combination kicked up a notch by a herbal tang that added a pleasant undertone of bitter.

'So,' he said. 'Now is where we'd normally find out a bit more about each other.'

'Hmm.' She studied his face, absorbed the sharp angles and strong planes, the intense blue of his eyes, eyes that held a depth she couldn't fathom. Knew she didn't want to lie to this man, not more than she already had, didn't want to make up a whole life story. So, 'I can't see the point. We're never going to see each other again, so does it matter where we live, what our jobs are? I'd rather know something else about you.'

'Like what?'

'Anything you want to tell me. About you. It doesn't have to be deep or meaningful, though it can be. It just has to be true.' She picked up her drink, swirled it round. 'So, for example, my favourite colour is red.' The red of the Saralan flag, though there was no need to explain that.

'OK. Something about myself.' He frowned and she wondered what he was thinking, feeling. 'My favourite season is spring.'

They paused the conversation as their pizzas arrived and then she resumed.

'My favourite music is jazz.' Another sign.

'Good choice.' He turned to look at the band that had just started to play. 'And lucky.'

They listened for a while, both of them caught up as they ate and she nodded. 'Yup. My foot's tapping and they play really well together. And this time I'm not making up information—my knowledge of jazz is a lot better than my knowledge on clocks.'

'You mean you had really never heard of the famous duck clock invented by Professor Mallard in the late fifteenth century, a precursor of the cuckoo clock because the good professor wasn't very good at recognising birds.'

'I believe Professor Mallard was a contemporary of Professor Woody who at the same time invented the woodpecker clock.'

'Or how about Professor Familio who invented the apparently famous great-great aunt clock?'

And then they were both laughing again, perhaps at the ridiculousness of the whole conversation, and all the made up clocks, perhaps because it felt good to laugh.

Marisa looked down at her nearly empty plate. 'I'm glad I tried something new.'

'So, it was a risk worth taking?'

'Definitely.'

'Want to take another?'

'Such as?'

'Shall we dance?'

'Dance?' she echoed, as the beat of the music carried across the room, the notes full of verve, carrying a beat of excitement, of speed, of risk and danger and an evocative sense of history and times gone by.

'Yup. I can dance, I promise. It was once a hobby of mine.'

Now her eyebrows rose. 'Truly? I'd have said you were more…' She couldn't help it, her hormones seemed to have taken this as a legitimate reason to let her eyes linger on his body, the breadth of his shoulders, the swell of muscle plain under the shirt, the solid wall of chest. She gulped, tried to cover her fluster by taking another sip of her drink. 'Maybe someone who works out.'

'Dance is a workout. But actually, I haven't danced in a while; this muscle is courtesy of sheer hard outdoor work. But I'm pretty sure it's like riding a bike. So will you take the risk?'

'Yes.' The agreement was instinctive, driven by a need to have a legitimate reason to get closer to him. Yes, it was a risk but she didn't care. There were other people on the dance floor—what was the worst that could happen? She'd spontaneously combust? It was a risk her hormones told her was worth taking. 'If I can put jackfruit on my pizza, I can do anything.'

'That's a good benchmark,' he said with mock seriousness as they both rose, and she smiled in response, but as they walked towards the dance floor the banter morphed into something else, a buzz of awareness, and a curiosity, a need to know what would happen to the zing of desire if they got closer.

And now they were suddenly, oh, so careful not to accidentally brush hands or bump arms. And then the music enticed them in and ensnared them in the beat and the tempo of the drums, caught them in the lingering notes of the saxophone. She realised that, somehow, they seemed to be in tune, able to read the music so that their steps moved together in something reminiscent of a Charleston. Dancing close and yet neither of them allowed any actual contact. Almost as if they were testing, teasing, tantalising, under the guise of a swing of arms, a shimmy of hips, the twist of a foot, their movements synchronised. Not touching somehow sparking a need, a growing shimmer of awareness.

Until the piece came to an end and they turned, both breathless and laughing. And still, oh, so close; all they would have to do was move forward an infinitesimal amount and she would be in his arms.

She felt frozen to the spot, and then the band started up again only this time it was a different tune, slow, dreamy, haunting, and he looked at her and what she saw in his eyes now made her clench with need.

The laughter was gone, instead there was an intention, a seriousness, and his blue eyes had darkened with a desire so real, so raw, that her tummy twisted in response, every synapse, every nerve taut now with a matching yearning, a craving so deep she caught her underlip in her teeth to stop herself from groaning out loud.

'Another?' he asked and she didn't even need

to reply, simply moved forward and now finally he was touching her, his hand against her waist, and she'd swear his touch branded her, burned with heat and warmth and promise.

The dance felt dreamlike, as if she were caught in a gossamer web of sheer physicality, every sense heightened to an elevated pitch, the beat of his heart beneath her fingers, the silky smoothness of his shirt, the sensitivity of her skin, the sound of the music a background noise that allowed them to be this close. The hard heat of his body pressed against hers, their movements completely attuned, the exquisite torture of being so close yet so far. Because on some level she knew they were in a public place, that when the music stopped, she would have to move away.

And when the last drawn-out note finally subsided she did just that, her head spinning, her whole body wrapped in a fugue of sheer desire and need, a longing she had to assuage. Because if she didn't take this opportunity, it would be gone, a chance not taken.

'Kieran?' His name was a breathless half-whisper. 'I...think we should leave.' Panic touched her he'd get the wrong idea. 'Together.' The word sounded desperate but she didn't care, hoped, *knew* he felt the same way.

'Together,' he repeated, his voice taut, yet

warm with assurance and husky with need as he held his hand out and she took it and they walked back to the table, together.

Somehow they got through the practicalities of paying the bill, the whole time her whole being clenched, as her brain tried to work, say things she knew had to be said. But first she had to know.

'Where shall we go?'

'Wherever's closest.' His voice was a half-laugh now as they exited the restaurant, still hand in hand.

'Good.' Relief touched her that she hadn't misread the situation.

'Where do you live?'

'Scotland.'

'That's no good.'

'No. But I'm staying in a hotel not too far from here.'

'That works.'

There were other things she knew she had to do, should do, before she could focus on this all-consuming desire. 'I'd better…'

'Call a friend.' Kieran nodded. 'I get that. And I need to make a stop at a pharmacy.' His voice was serious, the blue eyes intense, blond hair lit by a street light. 'I didn't plan this.'

'I know. I didn't either.' Her laugh was shaky.

'But this is our bubble of time, our night, and I want this. For this one night, I want you.'

'And for this one night I want you too.' The words sounded like a vow, felt momentous and now no more words were needed. He turned, headed for the nearest pharmacy and she pulled out her phone, texted Caro and then waited until he returned.

He took her hand again and now they walked, hands clasped, reached the hotel, headed straight across the lobby to the stairs, half ran to the first floor, where he fumbled with the keys, never once letting go of her hand and then they were inside and then she was in his arms.

His lips found hers and she knew she was lost, as desire zinged and flared inside her, and she fumbled with the buttons on his shirt, desperate now for everything, to kiss and be kissed, to touch and be touched, to get rid of any barrier between them. And then, somehow, they were on the bed and she could abandon herself to this vortex of desire, wanting to use every precious minute of the hours until the morning.

CHAPTER THREE

*Two months later,
the Indian island of Sarala*

MARISA SAT IN the throne room of the Saralan palace, tried not to focus on the glitter of the gilt-edged thrones, their solid, beautiful presence representative of power and justice and majesty. The very idea that she could one day sit on either throne seemed ludicrous, an idea she suspected her parents were trying to convey. 'Amma, Papa,' she murmured, tried to gauge their expressions, saw the familiar mix of love and confusion on her mother's face, reminiscent of all the arguments and rows as she had grown up.

'But this is what girls do,' had been the refrain that had echoed through the royal chambers. Along with, *'This is the way life is. You have to do your duty to Sarala. That means performing the duties of a princess.'*

But she had wanted to perform the duties of a prince, had believed that was her right. She was the eldest, she was just as capable as any boy, any male, any man. So, she hadn't wanted to learn the skills all women apparently needed. Didn't want to learn how to arrange tables, arrange flowers, choose an appropriate menu, wear the right clothes, didn't want to learn how to fade into the background. She wanted to be heir.

Something her parents had never been able to comprehend. They had treated her declaration to that effect with disbelief, and a disapprobation that verged on horror. A stance she felt was still in place, despite recent events, despite the fact that she now *was* the heir.

'Marisa, we have called you here to discuss your marriage.' As ever, her father went straight to the point.

Now her mother. 'This is something we need to sort out. The people are still very unsure about a woman being heir. The best way to reassure them is for you to marry and produce a son.' As though it were possible to choose.

'And reassurance is imperative.' Her father's voice was implacable. 'Remember Baluka.' Marisa did. The neighbouring island that had been a monarchy for so many centuries had now declared itself a republic. 'I will not allow that to happen here.'

Marisa knew her parents had a point. 'I understand, but I want to wait a little while, to make sure the people do understand that I am the heir, that it is I who will rule. If I marry now people may expect me to stand aside and let my husband take over.'

'Perhaps they will. In which case that is what you will do.' Her mother's voice was uncompromising. 'That is why you need a husband capable of doing that. A true ruler puts Sarala first. Above personal desires. That is something you have always had difficulty understanding.'

Marisa opened her mouth to protest, realised anything she said would sound like a series of self-justifications. Her mother's view was that Marisa had always been difficult, that her attitude stemmed from a disloyalty to Sarala's traditions. And then of course the debacle, the disaster with Lakshan, was something her mother still had not fully got over.

And that Marisa did understand, knew what she had done was unforgivable.

So, she held her tongue, tried to swallow the hurt that her parents didn't consider her capable of ruling.

'So right now, your duty to Sarala is to

marry the right man. We were thinking of either Prince Erik—he is European, of course, but that could make Sarala more of a global player—or Thakur Samir Munshibari. As the highest ranked aristocrat on Sarala, he understands our island.'

And would love the chance to rule it. Marisa bit back the thought. Both these names had after all been names she herself had considered. But that had been before. Before that night two months ago.

Images streamed into her brain. Pizza. Dancing. The lingering notes of a love song. The feel of cotton sheets. A hard body pressed against hers. Touch, heat, sensation, bliss…

Closing her eyes, she pushed the memory away. That had been one night. Her parents were talking about an alliance, a necessity, a lifetime of nights. Unbidden nausea threatened and she dismissed it as an overreaction. Her mother was right—she had to put Sarala first.

She bowed her head. 'I understand. But I need some time to think.'

She rose and as she did so a sudden dizziness threatened; she grabbed the edge of the table, met her father's concerned expression. 'I'm fine. I just need something to eat.'

'Look after yourself, Marisa.' Her mother's voice was laced with exasperation. 'You cannot afford to show any signs of weakness.' Her mother studied her. 'You also look pale. I know you don't like make-up, but appearance is important.'

Marisa nodded, needing to get out of the room before she did actually throw up. Ten minutes later she looked at her reflection in the bathroom mirror, realised her mother had a point. Opened the cabinet to check what medication was in there, scanned the back of a packet and froze as she read the warning. 'Do not take if pregnant.'

No…frantically calculating, she stared in horror at her reflection.

Scotland

Kieran ran a hand along the smooth, glossy wood of the newly installed staircase, a staircase he'd spent the past month designing and making, throwing himself into the project as though his very life depended on it. The month before that he'd dedicated to starting the garden, digging, loading, shifting soil, lugging bricks and concrete slabs, pushing himself to his physical limits. All in a vain attempt to forget one night, one woman whose image still haunted his dreams.

The ring of the doorbell distracted him and,

frowning, he headed to the window, peered out into the dusk of the Scottish evening and saw a small dark car parked outside.

None the wiser, he headed to the door, pulled it open.

'Hello. Can I help you?' He looked at the young, uniformed man standing on the door-step.

'Are you Kieran Hamilton?'

'Yes.'

'I'm here on behalf of the woman you know as Marina Carmody.'

Kieran blinked, ran the words through his head. 'Go ahead.'

'She needs to see you.'

For an instant an errant sense of happiness, jubilation and anticipation all combined to nearly put a smile on his face. One he suppressed instantly. One night had been the deal, one night he could almost justify as long as he didn't dwell on it.

But now… Here was this…summons?

'Why hasn't she contacted me directly?'

The young man's expression was wooden. 'I am not at liberty to say. She wishes to speak with you herself. She asked me to give you this.'

He handed over an envelope, and Kieran opened it, saw a simple embossed notelet within.

Dear Kieran
I need to see you, face to face. Amit will
bring you to me, if you agree.
* If you do not wish to come I understand,*
but please always remember I took a risk
and gave you this chance.
M

Kieran read the note twice and their conversation in the restaurant came back to him.
'There are consequences to risk,' she had
said. Was she warning him, telling him this
choice had risks attached either way? Or was
he reading too much into this? He could turn
away, go back into the house. Turn his back on
the woman he'd known as Marina Carmody.
Whatever that meant. Their deal had been one
night.

Or, 'So where would you be taking me?' he
asked, looked at Amit's expression and sighed.
'Let me guess…you're not at liberty to tell me.'

There was the smallest hint of a smile and
then Amit nodded. 'Exactly that.'

An image of her face in the restaurant, the
sparkle in her brown eyes when she'd told him
of her future plans, the feel of her body against
his on the dance floor, the strains of jazz, her
scent laced with the slightest hint of vanilla. The

strange sense of emptiness when he'd woken in the morning and she'd been gone.

He eyed the man she'd sent as her messenger. 'Are you at liberty to answer *any* questions?'

'No. Unfortunately not.' And Kieran had the feeling nothing was going to change that.

'Then let's go.'

'You may be gone overnight, so you may want to pack a bag. I am afraid I will need to take your phone and any other device such as a laptop until we reach our destination.'

Kieran hesitated and then shrugged. 'OK. I'll play along.' To his own surprise a sudden surge of anticipation and adrenalin fired inside him, a spark of curiosity and a desire to know what the hell was going on.

Ten hours later and he was none the wiser as the cargo plane taxied to a stop on a small airfield and, for a moment, he wondered whether he should be feeling a sense of fear—perhaps this was an elaborate kidnapping? Far-fetched, but then all of this was becoming increasingly surreal.

'So what now?' he asked Amit.

'You will be picked up from the airfield and taken to your destination.' The young man gave his first smile. 'I promise you, Mr Hamilton, there is nothing sinister happening. If you wish you can remain on the aircraft and I will return you to Scotland as soon as possible.'

'Having got this far, I'll see it through. I appreciate your flying skills.'

Twenty minutes later, he emerged from the aircraft, looked around as heat enveloped him, and he inhaled the smell of aviation fuel mixed with an exotic smell of flowers and greenery. He headed towards a small, dark, anonymous vehicle, climbed into the passenger seat and surveyed the driver, a young Indian woman, with short dark hair, and an expression that mirrored Amit's. She might as well be holding a placard saying *I am not at liberty to disclose any information.*

'Good evening. I'll get you to your destination as soon as possible.'

'Great. In the meantime, could you let me know what country I'm in?'

At first he thought she'd refuse, but then she answered. 'India.'

'Perhaps a little more information?'

'Sarala.'

Sarala… Sarala…the place name was not familiar, yet he had a feeling he'd heard the name recently. On the news, when he'd been half listening, his thoughts elsewhere. He wracked his brains during the trip, kept his eyes on the passing landscape, none of which gave him a clue, or triggered the elusive memory.

The journey continued and after a couple of attempts at questions that were met with expected rebuff, he descended into silence and watched as the car began a vertiginous ascent up a steep mountain road, which eventually flattened for a few miles before his driver turned onto a sweeping gravel driveway, flanked with lines of majestic dark-leaved verdant trees, leading to a sprawling whitewashed, two-storey colonial house, complete with stucco pillars.

Once parked, the driver turned to face him, her expression giving nothing away. 'Here you go,' she said. 'If you head to the front door, you are expected.'

'Thank you.' Kieran hoisted his bag onto his shoulder and climbed out of the car, as the front door opened and there she was. Marina. Or maybe not Marina?

He stood frozen as memories of that night flooded his brain: her face creased with laughter, lit with passion, her body entwined in his, pizza, dancing and then the cold space next to him in the morning. Enough. Right now, he had to work out what was going on, not allow attraction to blindside him. Again.

Forcing his legs into motion, he stepped forward. 'Hi,' he settled for.

'Hi. Thank you for coming. Come in.'

He entered to an impression of wealth and comfort combined. Wooden floors, polished and cool, covered in rattan rugs. Stone walls hung with a mix of pictures and tapestries.

Standing in the hallway, he studied the woman in front of him, saw she looked tired. Brown eyes shadowed, her forehead creased in a frown, body rigid with tension. A far cry from the relaxed, sparkling woman of two months ago. Abrupt concern touched him. Was she ill?

'Let's go through to the lounge,' she suggested and he followed her into a spacious room. The walls were painted a teal blue, the furniture antique but also comfortable-looking. She gestured to one of the armchairs and he stepped towards it, careful not to go too near her. Tried not to inhale deeply as the ridiculously familiar waft of her scent seemed to tantalise him.

'Please sit down.' Her voice stilted. 'Can I get you something to drink?'

'No, thank you. I'd prefer to know what is going on. As concisely as possible.'

'Of course. I apologise for the cloak-and-dagger stuff. I wanted to make sure you got all information directly from me.' She sat down opposite him, perched on the edge of her chair, then pushed herself backwards, straightened her back, took a deep breath, and a sense of foreboding started up in his gut, a knowledge that for whatever reason she had summoned him here, it wasn't for the pleasure of his company.

Eyes deadly serious, she met his gaze square on. 'I'm pregnant.'

The words ricocheted towards him, echoed, resounded, punched him in the solar plexus so hard he felt his breath catch, his lungs forgetting how to work, and instinctively he rose to his feet, paced to the window, not wanting her to see his expression.

Her statement mixing in his brain with the same words he'd heard from Aisla, delivered years before. His late wife's elfin face almost defiant as she'd made the same announcement, and now all he could think, all he could feel, was a surge of protectiveness. This time he would not fail. He would protect the tiny life growing inside the woman sitting in the upright chair. This woman, this stranger.

Those words permeated his brain, cut through the ravage of emotions and he turned around to face her. Back in control, at least on the surface.

'Are you sure?'

'Of course I'm sure. I didn't ask you to travel across the world on a whim.'

Her voice was tart and she had a point. 'OK, then. Are you sure the baby is mine?' He kept his voice steady, knew it was a question that had to be asked before he could process what to do next, work out what to feel. While he could still perhaps control the surge of protectiveness that lapped around the barrier of cold, hard common sense.

Now anger flashed in her eyes, a fire that sparked in those brown eyes and took him back to that now potentially fateful night, where her eyes had flashed with so many emotions: anger, laughter and desire. And he was back there, in the tangle of sheets, her body pressed against his, the silken feel of her skin, her hair, the touch...enough. That had happened. And this was the result.

Her fists clenched and then she took a deep breath, unfurled them and spoke. 'It's a fair question. You don't know me. So, you'll have to take my word for it. For now. When the baby is born, by all means, we'll do a DNA test. But right here and now I have decisions to make and I need to know: do you want to be involved in *your* baby's life?'

'Yes.' The answer came without thought,

propelled by the bone-deep knowledge that he would never let this child down. Would be there every step of the way. 'That is an absolute. I accept you have every right to make decisions about this pregnancy, but I will take the baby if...'

'If what?' Her expression was perplexed and then the frown disappeared. 'No. I am keeping this baby. That isn't what I meant. Though it's a fair assumption. Sorry. I'm not explaining things very well.' She paused, tipped her head to one side. 'But did you mean that? That you would take the baby—you can make a decision so life-changing that easily?'

'Yes.' He had no intention of elaborating, explaining that he'd lost one unborn child, that he'd already made the decision once to be a father. Had looked forward to it, planned it, imagined it. 'So now what?'

'Now I will tell you who I really am.'

Her gaze was steady and he tried to focus, everything already so surreal and yet he sensed that this revelation would tip his life further upside down. 'My full name is Her Royal Highness, Princess Marisa of Sarala.'

'Princess?' He could hear disbelief in his voice and, clearly, so could she.

Rising, she went over to a table in the corner

of the room, picked up a folder and brought it over to him.

Inside he found and opened a passport, scanned the picture, scanned the title and looked across at her. Pulled out the other contents of the file. Three newspaper articles all with pictures of the woman opposite him, all clearly captioned with the words 'Princess Marisa'.

'You may want to read the first article; it gives a fairly accurate summation of the situation on Sarala.'

Twenty minutes later he put the folder down and looked across at a woman he now knew to be not only a princess, but a princess who had just become heir to the throne of Sarala following the abdication of her younger brother, Rohan. A woman who would be the first female ruler in the history of her country, a history that spanned centuries of royalty.

'So, when you said you were going to take up a new job running the family business you were using some poetic licence.'

'Yes.'

'So this, all of this and you being who you are, how does this affect our baby? How does it affect your position? Clearly this is a minefield.' From what he had read, Sarala was a deeply traditional country, a place where the idea of a female ruler was in itself meeting with very mixed views. He suspected a pregnancy from a one-night encounter would be met with public outrage.

'That's why I asked you here. I have a proposal.'

'I'm all ears.'

'Actually, I mean that literally. I want you to marry me.'

The words slammed into him. 'Not possible.' The refusal was instinctive. How could he marry again? To do so would be a betrayal of Aisla's memory—he'd let her down in life, their marriage a roller coaster of emotion ending in tragedy.

'I understand I am asking a lot, but please will you hear me out?'

He inhaled deeply, tried to think against the fog of emotions swirling inside him. This was no longer about him. This was about a baby, an innocent being who had not asked to enter this world. But he or she existed now.

'Go ahead. I'm listening.' And he would; there was too much at stake here to allow his feelings to affect his concentration.

'In order for our baby to be able to succeed me as heir to the throne of Sarala, he or she, let's call her she, has to be born legitimately.'

'He or she?' he asked. 'Is that definitive? I

know they are changing the law to allow you to succeed but is that a one-off change?'

'I don't know,' she said, her lips twisted in a grimace. 'But regardless of that I will use all my influence, everything in my power, to ensure Sarala has a right of succession that means the oldest child is heir regardless of their sex. That's why I would like to refer to the baby as she, to remind me of how important that is and to make it clear that I will love this baby no matter what.'

Her words brought home to him how different traditions and culture must be on Sarala and how much it must mean to Marisa to be the first female heir in history. It also made sense of her next words.

'But, right now, the important thing is she must be born legitimately. That means I have to be married. To somebody.'

'So, we could get married for the sake of the piece of paper, then get divorced?' Even as he said the words, he sensed it would be more complicated than that.

'I thought of that but that wouldn't work. Sarala doesn't operate like that. I suppose it's like some sort of unspoken contract. As Royals we give our lives over to duty, to ruling, to doing our best for Sarala, and that means living a life that is scandal-free. And that rule applies doubly to females—it's not fair but it is how it is. And it will apply a thousand-fold to me as a female heir. My brother is divorced and that scandal rocked the throne. But we survived. Just. In the current political situation, we won't.' She shrugged. 'I mean maybe, possibly maybe, we may be able to divorce in the future, but I cannot guarantee it.'

'Maybe our baby won't want to be heir to Sarala. Maybe she will want to be a ballerina or a firefighter or a footballer? Maybe she wouldn't want us to get married just for her sake.'

'It isn't just for her sake.'

'What do you mean?'

'I cannot have this baby as a single mother—*that* scandal would bring the monarchy down.'

'What if you abdicate your position?'

'I can't do that.'

'Can't or won't?'

'Both. I don't want to abdicate.' Her hands clenched by her sides. 'I want to do this; it is my birthright and I love my country. I want to rule. I want to bring prosperity and happiness. I want to make Sarala into a true global presence. I want…oh, I want to do so much.'

He could hear the sincerity in her voice. See the spark of determination, of ambition, in her eyes. He recognised it as a look he'd once seen on his own face. A time when he'd been fired up by a desire to succeed, been driven to build profit, build sales, win funding, grow, go global, conquer the world.

'But it's more than that,' she continued. 'It's not only about what I want. I can't abdicate. If I abdicate so soon after Rohan that decision will most likely bring the monarchy to an end. There is no other close heir, male or female. Sarala will most likely follow its neighbouring island's path and become a republic. My parents would lose their crown, the knock-on effect may cause the other island in the triumvirate to follow suit. All traditions upturned because I made a mistake, took a risk too many, went on a date, had a one-night stand and fell pregnant. I won't let that happen. So, I can't *and* won't abdicate. So, I need to get married.

She stared at him, defiance shining in her brown eyes and the tilt of her chin. 'To you or to someone else.'

'Someone else? How would that work?'

'I haven't figured it out exactly.' Her voice was flat, taut with misery. 'But at least once I'm married, she will be legitimate and the throne will be safe. I would tell my husband the truth.'

'And where would that leave me?'

'As the man who turned me down.' Her brown

eyes met his, wide with pain, but also flecked with determination. 'I have to marry someone. It's your choice whether it's you or someone else. So, I'll ask again—will you marry me?'

CHAPTER FOUR

ONCE SHE'D ASKED the question a weight of sudden exhaustion descended on Marisa, along with a tsunami of doubts. Was this the best plan? She'd gone through this so many times in the past week as she'd tried to work out what to do, find a way forward. This was the best option, but it was also a risk. Now he knew the truth Kieran could literally destroy her, take her down and the monarchy with her.

There had been enough articles already, denouncing her as a princess who had spent the past ten years in exile and grown too far from her roots, was out of touch with her own country. This one-night stand, this pregnancy would show beyond doubt this was the case and would cause many to deem her doubly unfit to rule.

Further doubts shook her—was that true? Her own actions had caused her exile, her own choice had extended it, hers had been the deliberate decision to have one night of 'freedom'. Now her fate was in this man's hands. Sure, she'd tried to come across as the one with all the cards, hadn't given him a hint of her desperation or the extent of his power. But he wasn't a fool; he'd grasped the situation on Sarala in minutes.

He held her future in the palm of his hand.

Inadvertently her gaze flicked to the hand in question and, unbidden, a jolt of desire hit her, so intense she almost let out a gasp. She didn't need this now, couldn't let it mess with what was the most important conversation of her life. Yet it still took an effort to gather her refracted thoughts, to tear her gaze from his hand, to redirect it to his eyes.

Make one last pitch. 'I know what I am asking, know Sarala means nothing to you, know I mean nothing to you, but the baby is yours.' And he had been willing to have sole custody, be a single dad. 'If we get married, we will both be there every step of the way. Neither of us would miss out on any firsts, like first steps, first tooth.'

She had no idea what he was thinking, those intense blue eyes unreadable as he sat lost in thought. She sensed he was seeing something, thinking about something she couldn't fathom. But there was so much she didn't know about this man; in truth she knew nothing, yet she had risked her crown and her country by contacting him, by suggesting this path.

Eventually, after the silence had stretched her nerves to breaking point, his eyes met hers. 'There are so many reasons I could bring up why this is not a good idea, and in any other conceivable circumstance I would refuse. But I know that in any other circumstance you wouldn't propose this marriage. You have to get married to save the throne, the system of government, to give our child her birthright and keep your own. You didn't have to tell me about the baby, you could have married someone else, even passed this baby off as his.'

She wondered if even the smallest part of him wished she'd done exactly that and, as if he read her mind, he rose from his chair and came over to her. She rose so they were facing each other.

'I am glad you told me. I truly appreciate the risk you have taken in doing so and I am truly grateful you are giving me this chance to be a dad. If the options are that you marry someone else or marry me, then I choose the latter. I accept your proposal.'

Emotions swirled inside her; overwhelmingly relief that he had agreed, that the situation could somehow be salvaged. With the key word being somehow. This was just the first step and now panic entered the mix. So many questions and doubts and fears that her head spun, and almost before she could register the movement, steady hands had grasped her arms, his clasp firm and warm.

She looked up at him; the intense blue eyes focused on her somehow contained a wealth of reassurance and commitment and suddenly a whole new feeling shimmered into being, an awareness of his strength, of his closeness, his fingers on her bare arm, and now his eyes darkened slightly, oh, so reminiscent of how he had looked at her two months before.

Wild thoughts ricocheted round her head, and she felt an urgent need to focus on these feelings, to allow the strength of this attraction free rein so it could push away all the doubts and fears, assuage the panic. And as their gazes meshed, she knew he was thinking the same, that he wanted this as much as she did, wanted to block out the past and the future, just as they had two months before.

And she was back to that night, back to when life had seemed so full of promise, her dream within her grasp and the night a blissful, glorious moment in time where she'd found such joy, such intense pleasure with this man. The dizzy sensation of his lips on hers, his lips on her body, the look of awe in his eyes as he'd explored her. The strength of his muscles under her fingers, the texture of his hair. That sense of connection, that even now she could feel. And then, almost abruptly, he moved away, broke his hold, shattered the moment and the connection.

It was only then she even realised her eyes had been closed. Opening them now, she saw confusion and pain cross his expression, eyes shadowed and dark. But she could see more than that in them, could also see rejection and a sudden hurt panged through her, along with a jolt of pride.

What was she doing? This wasn't two months ago, because now they had a past and they had a future and this was a man who had power over her, a man who she was letting into her life for ever. And she didn't know him; what if he decided he wanted to rule? What if he decided to use his knowledge to manipulate her? What if he was another version of Lakshan, a man who had manipulated her, used her for his own devices, conned her and humiliated her? Not that she could let Lakshan take the full blame; she had allowed him to do that, handed him the power and the opportunity.

She wouldn't do that again; she'd already been forced to cede too much control, too much power. This near stranger would be her husband, would become a prince. She couldn't afford to let physical attraction become another potential lever he could use. And now she was thinking clearly again, it occurred to her to wonder if he had agreed to this marriage just a little too easily. Surely such a massive, life-changing decision should have warranted more thought. Or perhaps he was a man who was used to making decisions quickly, a man who could weigh up a situation and see the best outcome. Either way, did it matter? Whatever his reasons, the important thing was that he'd agreed.

She took a deep breath, saw that he too now had himself under control. 'Thank you for agreeing to this marriage. And apologies for just now; the enormity of it made me go a little shaky.'

'No problem. That is totally understandable.'

'You must be feeling a little overwhelmed yourself; neither of us could have foreseen this two months ago.' Even now she wondered how it had happened, could only surmise that a condom had split, or perhaps in the heat of the moment, one of the moments, maybe they had simply forgotten. 'Back then it was all about one night, a bubble where there was no past and no future.'

'Now it isn't,' he said. 'Two months ago, we didn't need to share anything about our lives, because it wasn't relevant. We thought we'd never see each other again. You could be Marina Carmody and I could be any generic guy out on a date. Now the people we are does matter—you are a princess.'

'And you,' she asked. 'Who are you?'

Kieran focused on pushing away the fuzziness engendered by the desire that still gripped him. It had taken every ounce of control he possessed to pull away from Marisa, his body rebelling against his brain's commands, wanting, needing to succumb to the heady desire, the pull of attraction. But they couldn't. He couldn't. Yes, he'd agreed to marry her. But he'd only done that for the baby. So he could be there to protect and love and nurture his child. No other reason. Their attraction, the connection that had sparked into an intensity that had stunned him, delighted him…that had been for one night and one night only. He had no intention of letting that attraction lead him into any form of emotional connection, and it would be unfair to pretend otherwise.

There was already the spectre of guilt, a sense that he was betraying his late wife and their unborn child. One night had led to another baby. Another chance. And now another marriage. It was too enormous to take in, generated emotions too big to encompass. A joy in the idea that there was a life forming. Guilt that he should be given another chance, one he didn't deserve. But alongside that was the overriding knowledge that the most important thing now was this baby.

He could see wariness in her face as she waited for his answer. She'd asked who he was.

'I'm the person I said I was—my name is Kieran Hamilton. What I didn't tell you is that I was married; my wife died in a car crash four years ago.' For a moment he was back there, hearing the screech of the brakes, seeing the approach of the lorry, his reactions as he reached out for the wheel, heard Aisla scream, as he desperately tried to swerve them out of the way, and then there was nothing but blessed darkness, numbness, until he woke up in a hospital bed. 'A lorry driver fell asleep at the wheel.'

Shock showed on Marisa's face and then she stepped forward, held her hand out as if to touch him and he instinctively moved backwards.

'I'm sorry.' She dropped her hand, her eyes wide as she looked up at him. 'So sorry.'

'It's fine.' As always, he could feel his whole

body tense with rejection. He neither wanted nor deserved sympathy. Another reason to not tell Marisa the whole story, about the baby who'd never been given a chance of life. He didn't want to see the pity, the compassion deepen. He didn't want to talk about it, his grief, his memories of that baby too precious to share. They were his and his alone, just as the grief and the guilt were his and his alone.

'No, it's not,' she said softly. 'But I get you don't want to talk about it.'

'No, I don't. But it's obviously a fact that you need to be aware of. It's also a fact that I know will have to become public.' Another reason to keep his baby private. He would not have his baby exposed to the media. It was unlikely anyone could find that out.

'Yes.' He couldn't tell what she was thinking, her face now as neutral as his own and he was grateful for that. Grateful that she wasn't going to ask questions, offer further sympathy. 'It will, but I will do all I can to make sure it is treated as sensitively as possible.'

'I appreciate that. Now I think we need to consider what happens next. I have a lot of questions.'

Her expression was suddenly sombre. 'I'm not sure I have many answers. But I'll try. How about we walk round the gardens? The eve-

ning is still warm and I could do with some
fresh air.'

A few minutes later as they stepped out
into the warmth of the evening Kieran looked
around, focused on the surroundings, tried to
ground himself in a place completely unfamiliar and as far a cry from Scotland as he could
be. The air was scented with a mixture of flowers that hung heavy yet pleasant in the breeze.
There was another smell as well, a sweet lushness he couldn't place.

As if reading his expression, she smiled.
'It's fig trees,' she said. 'I'll take you to them.
There's a part of the garden dedicated to them
and somehow the scent seems to be around
all year long. But you can probably also smell
mangos—there's a small mango orchard behind the house.'

'So where are we?' he asked. 'Is this your
home here on Sarala?'

'No.' She shook her head. 'This is a royal
retreat, up in the mountainous region. I told
my parents I needed some space to consider
my new position in the run-up to the coronation in two weeks. I came with Amit and
Jai. She's one of my security guards and the
woman who drove you here. Amit will return
here later tonight or tomorrow. There is a village nearby but this place is private enough

that it is unlikely you will be spotted, or at least not straight away.'

'Do your parents know about the pregnancy? Know about me?'

'No. My parents have told me I need to marry, to make a female heir more palatable to the people and also to produce an heir as soon as possible. They have offered me two possibilities, a European prince or a Saralan aristocrat. I think they believe I am considering these options while here.'

'So, I'm guessing a non-royal non-aristocrat isn't going to meet with unqualified approval? Or any approval.'

'Nope. Though if you happened to have a few million stashed away it may help, I suppose.'

'Well, actually...'

Marisa came to a stop, looked up at him. 'I was joking.'

Kieran shrugged. 'Actually, I am a millionaire.' Seeing she still looked lost for words, he continued. 'I am a partner in a creative agency called Mix It Up. We come up with innovative ways to promote businesses, films, people... For example, we were responsible for promoting season two of *The Oddness*.' A streamed science-fiction series that had captured the world's imagination.

'Seriously? You did that? I loved that series, but I also still remember the promotions. It was a fantastic idea.'

Kieran paused, recalling that time and the surge of adrenalin that had pumped through him back then. Fuelled perhaps as well by the grief that had still been so new and raw, the breakthrough coming a mere year after Aisla's death. A year where he had poured every ounce of energy into work.

'It was a make-or-break scheme.' The idea had been to carry out a series of choreographed 'odd' promotional stunts in a number of cities throughout the world, each stunt teased and anticipated across social media. 'The producers were dubious so we put some of the money in ourselves, because we knew it would work.' He remembered the buzz, the time, the effort. 'It did and after that the work poured in and we took off. Hence the millions.' Millions he had no interest in, had invested wisely and left to grow, unable to reap the benefits of a business that Aisla would never benefit from. He couldn't take the equivalent of what felt like blood money.

Marisa looked worried. 'How will that impact us? I mean, are you in the middle of a campaign?'

'No. I'm currently taking a sabbatical.' He

kept his voice light, had no intention of elaborating. 'I'm renovating a house in Scotland. It's
a project I can put to one side for now.' Only it
wouldn't be for now, he realised, it might well
be for ever. 'So, I'm all yours.'

Words that felt momentous and he hurried
on.

'And I have millions, which may make me
a more desirable prospect. Or at least it won't
hurt. Maybe that will make it easier to tell
them about us. About the baby.'

'We're not telling them about the baby.'

He turned to glance down at her, but she was
staring straight ahead, her lips pressed together
and her chin jutting out.

Kieran did a rapid calculation. 'But if you're
eight weeks pregnant, that means the baby is
due in seven to eight months and, more importantly, you may well start to show in the next
couple of months.'

Now she did look at him and he could see
surprise in her eyes. 'I know,' she said. 'But
I'm surprised that you do.'

It was the perfect opportunity to explain
the truth but, in that moment, Kieran knew
he wasn't going to. Not now, maybe not ever if
he could avoid it. Marisa didn't need to know.
This was his personal history, his grief, his
precious memory.

'My point is, your parents are going to figure this out, once the baby is born if not before.'

'Maybe, but I am still not telling them, or anyone right now. That's final and non-negotiable.'

'That's your call.' He sensed there were undercurrents here, things he didn't know and she clearly had no intention of explaining. Well, he got that. Her parents, her country, her business. But it still made no real sense, created a whole host of problems: 'In which case how are you going to justify marrying me, a man they've never heard of, rather than the prince or the aristocrat?'

'My plan *was* to say we've been together for a while.'

'That won't work.'

'I know that now.'

'Not because of my marriage. It wouldn't work regardless.'

'Why not?'

'A long-term relationship is too easy to disprove on a practical level. We have no photos, no proof. We haven't even lived in the same places. So, we need a different story, something we can sell.'

Marisa looked at him, her expression suddenly arrested. 'Like one of your PR campaigns.'

'That's not exactly what I meant.' It wasn't what he'd meant at all.

'It doesn't matter what you meant.' She came to a halt underneath a large tree and Kieran realised they'd reached the fig trees. He could see clusters of the red fruit bursting from the crooked trunk and branches, and he inhaled a scent reminiscent of spiced apples. 'That is exactly what we need.' Marisa's face was animated now. 'A campaign, a plan, and that's what you're good at.'

What he'd once been good at. Until his creativity, his drive, had vanished. His brain had stopped sparking, as guilt had torrented in. Aisla hadn't believed in his dream, had resented his drive and focus to achieve his ambition and that had soured their marriage, caused arguments and stress and made her unhappy. Then had come tragedy; Aisla died and then his company took off. A success she'd never see and that knowledge had engulfed and destroyed his creativity. 'I'm not good at that any more; I've been on a break for a while now.'

'But you could try.' He heard the plea in her voice and he understood it. She was fighting for her own survival, the survival of a monarchy and for the birthright of her child. Their child. Which meant he had to try and help, for the baby's sake.

Maybe it would help him too, be a way to distance himself from the emotional reality of events. He could treat this as a job, a campaign that would give him some space, a different perspective that would be easier to handle. Plus, how could he refuse to try?

So, back to basics. Rather than expect anything brilliant, start with the obvious. 'OK. You have to create an illusion, but you need to base it on a truth. You can't sell a chocolate bar as being full of nuts if it doesn't have any nuts in it. So, if we can't tell the truth about the baby, we pick another truth.'

'Such as…'

'We don't know each other very well so we tell everyone it's been a whirlwind courtship. That has an element of truth—you don't get a lot more whirlwind than a proposal after one date.' He could feel his brain begin to spin, to whir in ways it hadn't for a long time. 'It also covers the problem of providing proof of our dating life.'

'But why would we get married now? Why not just let our relationship keep going until we know each other better?'

'Because circumstances forced our hand. I was scared you would be persuaded to do your "duty" to marry the prince or the aristocrat, so I proposed.'

'And I agreed because…?'

'Because your parents have told you that you need to marry soon for Sarala.' His brain was beginning to think properly now, looking ahead, considering different options, different timelines. 'It is the "soon" that will be our biggest issue.'

Confusion touched her face and then he could see the penny drop with a clang. 'We will need to plan a big royal wedding, have a period of being engaged and by then the pregnancy will be obvious.'

'Exactly.' He hesitated. 'Are you sure you won't tell them you are pregnant?'

'One hundred per cent sure.' The steel in her voice told him that was an absolute.

'Understood.' Marisa was the client; her wishes held. 'In that case there is only one other solution.'

He felt the familiar sense of achievement, of finding the answer and knowing it was right. Now he just had to convince Marisa.

CHAPTER FIVE

MARISA SAW THE BRIGHTNESS, the triumph and the focus on his face and emotions mixed inside her. Hope that he had indeed found a solution, alongside a sense that events were slipping from her control. 'Let's keep walking,' she suggested, wanting to move, to ground herself in the lush royal gardens, a reminder of her status and position.

'Sure.'

She led the way, somehow taking reassurance from the soft crunch of the gravelled pathways, from the flanking landscaped bougainvillea hedges that exuded a soft floral scent, a miasma of violet overtones from the vibrant red and purple flowers. She came to a halt when they reached a mosaic-tiled courtyard area and she gestured to a bench. 'Shall we sit?'

Kieran nodded, followed her to the circular wooden table, surrounded by a cushioned bench. Once seated, Marisa gazed around at the water features, beautiful, graceful yet solid stone bowls dotted around the area, listened to the soothing notes of the water that curved upwards and back down, inhaled the scent of lavender that grew in profusion in an array of terracotta pots. Then turned to Kieran. 'OK. Tell me. What is the solution?'

He didn't hesitate. 'We present your parents, everyone, with a *fait accompli*. We get married first, and tell them after.'

Any sense of calm engendered by their surroundings vanished. 'Not possible. That idea is off the wall and bouncing. I'm a princess; I can't go and get married without telling anyone.'

He shrugged. 'Fine. Then we'll have to wait.'

'But we can't wait.'

'Exactly.'

She opened her mouth and closed it again. 'It won't work. How can we possibly justify getting married in secret?'

'Not secretly. *Privately.*' He drummed his fingers on the table. 'We get married privately because we don't want to upstage the coronation. That is the ceremony that is most important and when you take on that responsibility you want to be married. And on your way to providing an heir.'

The enormity of marrying without her parents' knowledge was almost impossible to compute. But weighed against that was the equally impossible. That her parents should find out that she was pregnant—that she had been reckless enough to nearly overset the monarchy by providing fodder for an onslaught of scandal it would be unable to survive. They would never get over the disappointment of that, would never trust her to rule. Might try to find an alternate solution.

'It's not ideal but it's all we've got. So, we do it and we sell it.' His voice held reassurance and understanding. 'Not every client has a product that's easy to sell, but if I believe in it, I'll find a way.'

'So, you believe in our marriage?'

'I would never promote something I didn't believe in. A lot of people believe that advertising is the same as lying; I don't. I believe in this marriage because it is the best way for me to be there for my child, to be part of her life. Why do you believe in it?'

'Because it is necessary to safeguard my child's birthright and safeguard the monarchy.'

'Good. So we both believe in this marriage.' She could hear the confidence in his voice. 'That's the first step. Don't look so worried.... this was your idea remember?'

'I know it was my idea, but now I don't see

how we can pull it off. How can we make people believe in a whirlwind courtship? It didn't exist! The only real reason you would propose and I would agree is for love. And that *is* a lie.'

Kieran had wanted one date, was a widower, loved his wife, hadn't been ready for a second date, let alone a marriage. Yet he had agreed to it and again a sudden doubt entered her mind as she thought about all he would be giving up. What about his company, his work, his house…his life? Would he regret the loss of all of that, regret the sacrifice he was making for the sake of his baby? Yet looking at him now, he seemed so fired up, so sure of himself that it would surely be foolish of her to question anything? It wasn't as though she wanted him to change his mind, so, instead of speaking, she listened as he waved a hand for emphasis.

'It's an *illusion* that we need to create.'

'That's advertising semantics.'

'Perhaps. But it's true. In the same way that *The Oddness* was a spectacular show. Was it the best science-fiction show ever? That's a matter of opinion. But our mission was to present it as such, to persuade people to watch it, to give it a chance. That's what we want here: people to give us a chance. If we need to create an illusion of love, then so be it.'

'But how can we do that? *The Oddness was* a spectacular show.'

'And our night together was spectacular. We are going to use that to build on.'

'How?' She could hear the hint of hysteria in her voice and gritted her teeth.

'We are going to figure out our first date, our illusory one. Think back to that night. The feeling you had when we first saw each other, when we were stuck in that blasted door.'

Marisa looked back, recalled the instant jolt of awareness, could see the outline of his hand pushing against the bar of the door, recalled his scent, his bulk and then the realisation that he was her date.

'OK. Now let's move the scene a bit. Assume our date was set up by friends in a more usual way—let's say you know my friend and business partner, Lucy, and she set the date up, a few months ago.'

'Early November? I was in London then.'

'Perfect. So where do we meet? What are we doing? Something quite generic, nothing that can be proved or disproved.'

'Something fun and something normal.'

'A date for Marina Carmody not Princess Marisa. It would have been autumn, leaves turning red, a nip of cold in the air but not woolly-hat-and-coat weather.'

'We went roller skating in the park. Or for a long walk, crunching leaves, we're holding a hot chocolate, maybe pumpkin-spiced.'

'We're walking and talking and laughing. I tell a joke about clocks and it feels ridiculously funny. We're breathless with laughter and we find ourselves holding hands.'

Marisa felt as though they were there, his voice so mesmerising that, instead of the heat of a Saralan evening, she'd swear she felt a breeze redolent of the scent of autumn in London, mixed up with a memory of their date, of genuine laughter.

Without even realising it she'd moved around the bench in the here and now, the warm, muscular bulk of his body right next to her, and his hand brushed against hers and she heard her own sharp intake of breath.

'We're at the end of the walk,' he said.

'But we don't want to say goodbye yet. I see a funfair in the park and we decide to go there.'

'We go on the scariest roller coasters, and there is so much adrenalin.'

'We eat hot dogs.'

'And candyfloss. And by the time we're done it's dark and we still don't want to say goodbye.'

'There is a firework display. We go to that.'

She could almost hear the crackle and fizz

of the fireworks, feel the warm bulk of Kieran next to her, smell the mulled wine, hear the gasps as a rocket shot through the sky in a blaze of colour against the midnight blue and then exploded above them.

'And as the fireworks explode over our heads all I want to do is kiss you and as if you sense it you turn to look up at me and...'

And somehow it was so real and the pretend then and the real now all fused together and they'd turned to face each other and then he kissed her, or maybe she kissed him, she didn't care. Because now fireworks of a different sort were going off inside her as fantasy and reality merged and she gave a small gasp of pleasure as he deepened the kiss and then she was lost. Her body pressed against his, her arms around his neck.

Until the caw of a bird broke through, a sound she recognised, a sound that grounded her, reminded her exactly where she was and she pulled away, slid away from him, rose to her feet, her head spinning. And now mortification set in, along with an anger directed at herself.

What was she doing? She had no idea why he'd kissed her. Had it been part of his campaign, a calculated decision, a practical demonstration of how to create an illusion? Or had he too been carried away in the moment? She didn't know and in some ways it didn't matter. She could not and would not let attraction dictate her actions. Would not show weakness or vulnerability, would not give this man a power over her in the same way she had given it to Lakshan. Would not allow him to use attraction to mess with her head, put judgement and common sense aside.

Because that was to court disaster. This man would be by her side; to give him power over her gave him power over Sarala and she would not do that.

'Sorry. That shouldn't have happened.' She managed a smile. 'For a minute there I believed the story. Which I assume was the idea.'

There was a beat of silence and she wondered what he was thinking, what he was feeling.

Then he too stood up. 'Yes, that was the idea; to take the theme from our real date and make it into a more sellable version. Because there were fireworks. Our date, our bubble of time, was full of metaphoric fireworks and we can use that to sell us as a couple. It's about believing the story, about making it real.'

Marisa straightened her shoulders, determined to match his matter-of-fact manner, determined not to show that the kiss had dizzied her head, wobbled her legs and been a lot more than a calculated attempt to make the illusion real.

'That makes sense. We've taken some of the truth from our real date and woven it into a what-might-have-been, and we've made that might-have-been feel real.' She met his gaze firmly. 'And the fireworks. You're saying we should use our attraction to help create the illusion of love?'

'Yes. Because the attraction exists.'

Even if the love didn't. He didn't say the words but he didn't need to. She knew the love didn't exist. Knew it never would. And that wasn't a problem. She had been brought up to know her duty would be to make a political marriage. Apart from that one time when she'd been foolish enough to think love existed, but instead had been hoodwinked and lulled into near disaster and a morass of humiliation. After that she'd known her marriage had to be dictated by logic, had to be an alliance.

So, love didn't come into it. Their attraction existed but it was nothing but a physical reaction, a scientific thing, just like fireworks. Fireworks that lit the sky up for a few minutes at great cost and then died away. That was a lesson she'd already learnt.

'Agreed.' She started walking again, wanted

the physical exercise, a way to expend the energy that had been created by that kiss, the after-effect still strumming through her body.

He walked beside her, but she noted he was as careful as she was to keep a distance between them. 'Now we need to figure out the logistics of getting married. Is it possible to get married here in the next few days or are there legal reasons that it takes longer? In England you have to give twenty-eight days' notice.'

'Not here,' she said. 'All we have to do here is get a pandit, a celebrant, to carry out the ceremony. I will have to ask Amit and Jai to help but I can trust them.'

'What about your brother?'

'I don't want to involve him. His relationship with my parents is complicated enough right now. I don't want to ask him to lie for me.'

'Then we'll keep it simple. Arrange the ceremony for as soon as possible. The sooner the better.'

The sooner the better, for better or worse. The phrases raced round her head, threatened panic even as she nodded agreement.

'I'll talk to Jai and Amit tonight.'

CHAPTER SIX

KIERAN OPENED HIS eyes two days later knowing that this was an important day. As he looked up at the unfamiliar bright white of the ceiling, at the fan that whirred round and round, heard the caw of birds from the open window, it all came back to him.

Three days ago he'd been in Scotland, now he was on Sarala, his whole life transformed. He was going to be a father; he was going to be a husband. Memories, emotions, disturbed images from dreams he couldn't remember threatened and he sat up, all too aware of the utter surrealness of the situation. Awed at the idea of the baby growing inside Marisa, guilt-ridden as he remembered the baby he'd lost. He had a sense of an unexpected future versus the bleak knowledge that for Aisla and their baby there was no future.

Rising, he walked to the window, needing to ground himself. The past two days he'd barely had time to think, immersed in planning the ceremony, exactly as he would have planned a promotional campaign. Looking at the big picture and the finer detail to ensure it would all work.

Today he would marry Marisa, the woman he had spent weeks trying and failing to banish from his mind. In hours they would make vows that would bind them together. Kieran inhaled the already warm early morning air and looked out over the lushness of the landscape. The vibrant green of the frondlike branches of the palm trees with their knobbly slender trunks. The burst of flowers that sent out a wave of exotic smells. A whole new world, a whole new start.

One he hadn't anticipated or even wanted. He recalled the morning of his first wedding. Knowing then that Aisla's parents hadn't thought him good enough. He'd also known that his own parents had their doubts, though they'd kept them to themselves.

But he hadn't cared and neither had she... They'd been so sure of their happy ever after. Thought they'd known each other. It had been only a year into their marriage when it had become clear that they hadn't.

Now here he was embarking on a marriage with a woman he barely knew at all. A woman he intended to make a life with, a future with, so that he could be a good parent, could give his child love and security and her birthright. But he also intended to be a good husband. Doubts twisted inside him; he'd already failed to be a good husband to Aisla despite all his good intentions. What if he wasn't capable?

He shook his head. Enough. This time would be different. This was a marriage of convenience. A contract. There would be rules in place, the bar of expectation set at a reasonable height. The terms understood by both parties.

He turned from the window and headed for the bathroom, allowing his mind to return to the plan, the campaign, the ceremony itself. He ran through the types of photos, how things would be released to social media, his plan for promoting himself as the right man to marry a Saralan princess. All the things that released a buzz of adrenalin that dislodged any lingering doubts.

He emerged from the shower to a knock at the door. He knew it would be Amit as arranged, come to accompany him to the flower market. He called, 'Come in,' and turned with a smile that fell from his face as he saw the man who followed Amit into the room.

'I'm sorry.' Amit met his gaze with an expression of apology, defiance and determination combined. 'I couldn't help with this wedding without telling Rohan. So here he is.'

Kieran surveyed the man facing him, could see the resemblance to Marisa in the aquiline jut of the nose and the shape of the eyes. Eyes that held anger, disdain and a contempt that raised Kieran's hackles.

Yet he understood that Rohan would be bound to have doubts and so he held out his hand and, after a pointed hesitation, Rohan briefly grasped it.

'Good to meet you.'

'Is it?' Rohan asked, the edge in his voice clear.

'Yes. You're Marisa's brother. I know how important you are to her.'

'Not important enough to be told about, let alone invited to, her wedding. Not important enough, in fact, to even have been told about your existence, though according to Amit you have been seeing my sister for months.' Rohan's voice was flat, bitingly taut with anger.

'That was Marisa's decision and one I respected.'

'If you had any respect for my sister you wouldn't be trying to marry her behind her family's back. Well, that is not happening. I am here now to put a stop to this wedding. To rescue my sister from a mistake she will regret.'

Amit stepped forward. 'Ro, hold on. That's not why I told you about this.' He frowned. 'Does Elora know what you are doing?'

'Elora knows that I am here,' Rohan said.

'Does she know that I told you this because I thought you should be at your sister's wedding?'

'And I agree,' Kieran said. 'Or at least I did. Now I am beginning to see Marisa's point. Your sister does not need rescuing and if she did, she is quite capable of rescuing herself.'

Rohan raised his eyebrows, his features cold, his entire stance supposed to intimidate. 'So, you expect me to believe it is coincidence? A cloak-and-dagger wedding just months after my sister becomes heir to the throne? It is clear that you are after her wealth and her position; fancy yourself as a ruler, do you?'

Kieran stepped forward, anger racing through him, heating his blood, and Rohan did the same.

'Stop!' Amit moved in between the two men, clearly unfazed by the fact Rohan was a prince. 'Ro, you're overreacting. And a brawl isn't going to help matters.'

Kieran forced himself to step back, though his fists remained clenched by his sides. He tried to remind himself that Rohan was simply being a protective brother. 'Amit is right. So instead of a punch-up, why don't you listen? Your abdication caught us by surprise. Marisa and I were keeping our relationship under wraps to avoid publicity. Then she became heir and your parents are pressuring her to marry. A political marriage to Prince Erik or Thakur Munshibari.'

There was a silence and he could see he had caught Rohan's attention.

'I won't stand aside and watch Marisa be persuaded or guilted into a political alliance she doesn't want.' And he meant that, sensed that there was a vulnerability about Marisa despite her strength. That when it came to duty she could be manipulated, could be persuaded that her duty lay where her inclination didn't. Well, not on his watch. 'Your sister shouldn't marry to please her parents or her country.'

Kieran could see emotions shadow the Prince's eyes and he felt a pang of sympathy. It couldn't have been easy to step down. He couldn't even begin to imagine the ramifications, the risks, the heart wrench that must have gone into the decision.

'I will do my best to stand by her and support her in her new role.' He paused. 'A role I know she wants, a role she wishes to fulfil to her best potential and I admire that. But I also believe she should marry the man she wishes to marry.'

'You.' The word said with a hint of scepticism, surprise, but with less heat than before.

'Yes. Me. I hope you will stay today. I hope you will be part of this ceremony. I know how important a part family plays in a traditional Saralan wedding and I am sure Amit is right, it will mean a lot to Marisa if you are there.' He stepped backwards, glanced at his watch. 'But either way I have a list of things that need to be done before this afternoon.'

He held Rohan's gaze, waited as the other man stood immobile, no trace of his thoughts on his face.

Then he nodded. 'I'll be there. And I'll help as much as I can. I owe Marisa that much,' he said. 'But if you hurt my sister in any way, you'll have me to deal with. Is that understood?'

'Understood.'

Rohan's phone beeped and he looked down, gave a sudden smile. 'Elora is here,' he said.

Marisa stood and stared at her reflection, wished she knew how she was feeling. This wasn't how she had expected her wedding day to be and for a minute sadness touched her. Sadness that her parents weren't here, that there weren't all the traditional build-up and ceremonies. Not that it mattered—what mattered was that she was getting married, her baby would be legitimate, would have her birthright.

Nothing was more important than that. Not even Kieran? The question slipped unbidden into her mind. He too was getting married, had upended his whole life at the drop of a hat. How was he feeling right now?

She turned as she heard a frantic knock on the door, barely had time to shout come in before Jai burst in.

'Kieran texted me. Amit, the traitor, has told your brother about the wedding. Rohan is with him and Elora is...'

'Elora is here,' came a voice from the door. 'No way was I leaving Rohan to manage this; he may be a seasoned diplomat, but I feel he may not be at his most ambassadorial in these circumstances.'

Marisa turned as her sister-in-law-to-be entered the room, impressed as she always was by Elora's calm, serene demeanour. Dressed in her favourite teal, the blonde princess positively glowed with a radiant happiness. A happiness that had surrounded her ever since she and Rohan had finally admitted they loved each other.

'He assured me that he will deal with Kieran, but I came to make sure you aren't in the line of his fire.' Elora smiled. 'I know you are perfectly capable of standing up for yourself, but he is in full brother mode. Mostly because he is still worried he has burdened you with being heir.' She approached Marisa. 'And now I'll stop talking and let you say something.'

Marisa knew Elora had been speaking to give her time to collect herself and she was grateful for that. She knew how perceptive Elora was, knew she must not suspect the real reason for this marriage. And at least now her doubts were at rest; Kieran was being given the perfect opportunity to back out of this marriage and it sounded as though he wasn't.

'What do you want me to say?' she asked.

'Is this marriage what you want?' Elora asked.

'Yes.' That was easy.

'Do you trust the man you are about to marry?'

Marisa opened her mouth to answer, saw the gravity in Elora's expression and knew the other woman wouldn't believe a rushed answer. 'I haven't known him that long so perhaps the most truthful answer is that I hope I can trust him.' She placed a hand on Elora's arm. 'I understand why you have concerns but I promise this is the right thing to do. Amma and Papa want me to marry Prince Erik or Thakur Munshibari. I don't want to do that, but...'

'You are worried you will be persuaded to do your duty.' Elora's voice held true understanding. 'As I was. I was lucky with Rohan.'

'But you didn't already have another man in the picture, someone you did want to marry.'

Elora inhaled deeply and, though her eyes still looked troubled, she gave a decisive nod. 'OK. I will trust you. As long as Rohan hasn't discovered something about Kieran.'

She pulled her phone out and walked from the room, returned a few minutes later.

'Let's get this show on the road.'

Marisa smiled; the idea that she would have Elora by her side was uplifting. This was her wedding day and the only one she planned on having. Maybe it was all an illusion, maybe there was no love involved but, still, she wanted Kieran to look at her and have one awestruck moment.

'Let's do this,' she said.

Three hours later Kieran stood ready in the courtyard of the royal residence, shielded from the possibility of publicity by the sheer scale of the royal gardens.

Rohan was standing next to him and he felt

that, while Marisa's brother wasn't exactly happy with the course of events, he was willing to suspend judgement, assisted by the telephone conversation he'd had with Elora.

Swiftly Kieran's mind ran over all the plans. He hoped he'd got everything right, that it would all work, look right in the photographs he'd asked Amit to take for social media. Hoped too he looked all right, that Marisa would approve. He had wanted to show that he was embracing Saralan culture and tradition without trying to pretend he was someone he was not. So, he'd opted for the traditional long shirt worn by Saralan grooms. The pale gold linen with its high neck and embroidered cuffs was surprisingly comfortable, worn over a pair of his own lightweight cream trousers.

Then the door opened and Marisa came out and all mundane thoughts fled as his eyes rested on his bride and time seemed to be suspended.

He was vaguely aware she was flanked by two women, but his gaze focused solely on Marisa. He couldn't look away as he stood, mouth agape, feet frozen to the ground, mesmerised by her sheer beauty.

The white and gold sari edged with red shimmered and caught in the sunlight, her glossy black hair was woven with white flowers and cascaded in smooth waves to her shoulders. Her face glowed with a radiance and a strength of beauty that seemed timeless, and he knew this vision of her would be etched on his memory, this instant in time captured as she walked towards him. Every detail embedded in his memory banks: the golden strappy sandals, the glitter and jangle of the bangles that adorned her slender arms and glinted in the sunshine.

His breath caught and he blinked as Rohan nudged him in the ribs and he recalled what he was supposed to be doing. He walked towards the *mandap*, a wooden structure that would act as the altar. One part of his brain focused on making sure it looked exactly as he had left it, adorned and decorated with Marisa's favourite flowers that he'd picked up from the market that morning—a brilliant sweet-smelling cascade of red and white interwoven with greenery decorated each wooden pillar. In addition, there were strands of golden bells that chimed in the light afternoon breeze.

He stepped up onto the platform, Rohan still beside him, until he was seated on one of the velvet cushioned chairs. Then Rohan stepped off and Marisa started to walk towards the *mandap*, flanked by Jai and Elora, who both carried *diyas*, small hand-held lamps whose flames burned brightly, shimmering red in the sunlight.

Marisa walked with regal grace, her steps in perfect time to the music. It was a traditional Saralan wedding composition played on the *nadaswaram*, the oboe-like instrument creating notes that lingered and rested on the heat-laden air, permeated with the scent of the flowers. Everything combined to create an aura of solemnity and magic, laden with meaning. And as he watched his bride head towards him, so beautiful, so precious, awe and admiration mingled inside him.

Her gaze met his as she stepped onto the *mandap* and he hoped his eyes conveyed his feelings. Her face flushed a little as she gave him a small, sweet smile and then she sat next to him, the silk of her sari brushing his skin with a sensuous sweep of material. He inhaled her scent that mingled with the flowers and now a low hum of desire also pervaded the air, a sweet, sensuous awareness of the woman next to him. The woman about to become his wife.

Now the pandit, a small grey-haired man with twinkling brown eyes, carefully lit a small fire in the fire pit in front of them. Kieran watched the flames dance and flare, knew from his research that the fire was seen as a purifier, a sacred sustainer of life, and that vows made in its presence were binding.

The pandit surveyed them with a hint of curiosity but also with solemnity as he indicated they should rise. They faced each other over the fire, Marisa held her hands out and now he could see the henna tattoos more clearly, a kaleidoscopic picture of intricate swirls and shapes. He took her hands in his and, as he'd been shown, they walked around the fire as the pandit spoke and they repeated their vows in the Saralan tradition.

Then Rohan stepped forward and spoke softly to the pandit, who nodded. Rohan moved towards them and, kneeling before them, he carefully placed seven stones in a row on the ground.

Kieran turned to Marisa in question; this wasn't something he had been expecting.

'It represents seven vows or promises,' she said softly. 'We step from stone to stone and touch each one with our foot.'

'As your brother I wish you happiness in this lifelong commitment,' Rohan said.

'As your sister I thank you.'

Then, taking Kieran's hands, she led him to the stones and the pandit began to speak verses in a language that washed over Kieran, and although he didn't understand them he sensed their solemnity and importance as they touched their toes to each stone.

Then it was over and they stood back, waited as Elora and Rohan came forward and handed them both garlands of flowers. Gently he looped his around Marisa's neck, his fingers brushing the bare skin on her shoulder, and he felt her shiver in response. Then she put a garland round his neck, stood, oh, so close, and the heady scent of the flowers, the scent of Marisa, made his gut clench with a sudden desire.

He gazed down at her, almost lost in the depth of her brown eyes, and saw so much there. The realisation that they were married, that they had committed themselves to each other, that they were already bound by the baby growing inside her.

'We did it,' he said softly, both her hands clasped in his now, wanting to keep her close.

'We did it,' she repeated.

Then he saw her glance across to Rohan, who was standing with Elora, saw that the couple were holding hands, saw Elora look up at Rohan, saw the return gaze and saw love, a love he sensed was forged and bonded and real. And he could see a sudden sadness in Marisa's eyes, one he wanted to banish. Perhaps they didn't have love, but he knew that there were more important things than love.

He and Marisa would have constancy and security and they did have fire and passion and he wanted to remind her of that.

'Now it's time for another tradition,' he stated and smiled down at her, saw sadness disappear and anticipation take its place, a spark of desire as he bent his head to kiss her. The feel of her lips, smooth and glossy with a hint of cherry, her hands letting go of his so she could loop them round his neck, and he deepened the kiss for a moment, then a glorious moment more, until he heard someone clearing their throat and remembered that this was a wedding and kissing the bride was not a Saralan tradition.

He pulled back, blinked in an attempt to disperse the fugue of desire, to prevent himself from pulling her back into his arms, saw the same burn of need in her eyes before she too blinked and stepped backwards.

She turned to face the pandit, thanked him for his services and for respecting their privacy and confidentiality. Then Rohan and Elora stepped forward.

'We will leave you now, too,' Rohan said. 'But I will come with you to tell our parents of this marriage.'

Marisa shook her head. 'No. They will be upset you didn't tell them.'

'That doesn't matter. I am happy to stand by and explain my decision to them.'

'I understand that,' Kieran put in. 'But I don't want your parents to think I am hiding behind you. I too will stand by my decisions and my actions.'

'You would feel the same if it were my parents,' Elora said softly.

'Very well.' Rohan nodded. 'But please feel free to mention the fact we attended the wedding. And now I think it's time we went.' He stepped forward and as he gave his sister a hug, Kieran could see the genuine love there.

A few minutes later Rohan and Elora had gone, taking the pandit with them, Amit and Jai had melted discreetly away and he was alone with his bride.

On their wedding night.

CHAPTER SEVEN

MARISA TURNED TO KIERAN, her husband… The word seemed impossible—the whole day was still tinged with an aura of unreality, illusion and magic mixed to create the trappings and sense of a momentous occasion. And now here they were…alone…and she didn't know what to say; her mind was still blitzed by their kiss. A kiss she wanted to believe was real, but she had no idea if it had been part of the show, and that realisation made her keep her distance.

Because this was how it had been with Lakshan. She had believed his kisses were real, that they represented love, commitment, genuine emotion and feelings. But those kisses had been meaningless, each one a calculated assault on her senses, designed to dupe and deceive.

She could acquit Kieran of duping her. In this case she was a knowing, willing accomplice in her own deception. So it was time to step back.

The very fact that she was foolish enough to want their kiss to be real should trigger warning bells. An alarm she needed to heed.

But, illusion or real, she also knew what she owed him.

'I want to thank you. For today. For all the effort you put in to make this day special and the way you embraced our traditions and culture. I know it had to be done, I know it was part of the campaign, but you made it more than that. My favourite flowers, my favourite composer. The day was magical and that was thanks to you.'

'I'm glad,' he said simply. 'And it wasn't just for show, it was for us. This whole day, the ceremony, the traditions behind it all…it bowled me over. You bowled me over. When I saw you walk out, I was transfixed…you looked, you *look*… truly beautiful, Marisa.'

She felt a surge of pride, of joy even that she'd achieved that. 'Then I'm glad too.'

He looked towards the *mandap*. 'The stones that Rohan put down, tell me about them.'

'They represent the first steps of our married life and each stone is a promise,' she said. 'I didn't know Rohan was going to do that; I think he was reminding me of the gravity of what I am doing. I'm sorry that you had to make those vows blindly, that I didn't have a chance to tell you what they meant.'

'Tell me now.'

'They are what we need to take into our marriage with us, as we step through life together. We have to have mutual respect, to try and prosper together and share our wealth and our achievements, raise strong, good children, be faithful, be lifelong partners, work together to create balance between the mental, spiritual and physical. Acquire happiness and harmony through mutual love.' She gave a small smile. 'It's a lot to ask on a few days' acquaintance.'

'But it's not a lot to ask from a marriage,' he replied. 'You thanked me for arranging the wedding, but I want to thank you. You gave me this chance, this opportunity to be a father and to be part of my child's life. You didn't have to do that—you took a big risk and I promise you I will do everything I can to make sure you don't regret it. I will be a good dad.'

She could hear the sincerity in his voice and she was glad, deeply glad to know how much he already loved their child. But despite herself, despite everything she knew, her upbringing, her disbelief in fairy tales, a tiny part of her didn't want his gratitude, she wanted his...

His what, Marisa? Love?

That was ridiculous. So, she smiled, hoped

the smile hid her sheer nonsensical thoughts. 'You don't have to thank me. As for risks, I told you, if I can put jackfruit on my pizza, I can do anything.'

That pulled a smile from him. 'That definitely set the risk bar pretty high.' He took her hands in his and she felt the all too familiar tug of desire in her gut, even as she appreciated the words he was saying. 'Those vows... I'm happy to sign up to most of that. I believe in respect and sharing. I want to raise our child or children to the very best of my ability, to love them and be there for them. I intend to be faithful and I am in this for the long haul. And I want to make you happy.'

'What about you? You must want happiness for yourself?'

There was a silence and she felt his body stiffen slightly at the question, almost wished she hadn't asked it.

Then, 'Of course I do,' he said lightly. 'And I intend that *we* will be happy. Starting now. I have a wedding dinner planned. We may be the only guests but that doesn't mean we shouldn't celebrate.'

The fleeting question crossed her mind as to whether this was just another story he was creating, a memory to share with the media, an illusion made real, and she banished it. Right now, it didn't matter. The reality was that they were married and he wanted to celebrate that fact. That was a good thing.

'I will quickly go and change. I don't want to drop food on my wedding sari.'

'Good plan. I'll do the same. And, Marisa?'

'Yes?'

'This isn't part of the illusion. This is real. It's our wedding night and I want it to be special. Not a story we are creating, but a real-life story we are living. So, tonight is whatever we want it to be. Whatever you want it to be.'

His voice rippled over her skin, held promise and anticipation and brought back a swirl of memories of their night together. The sensations, the soaring joy, the reckless abandonment to pleasure, the breathlessness, the laughter and the sheer satisfaction.

Whatever she wanted it to be... How could she possibly work that out?

'Hold that thought,' she said, barely recognising her own voice.

'I will.'

Five minutes later Marisa looked at her reflection, tried to see if she looked different now that she was married. Married. She closed her eyes, reminded herself that this was a marriage of convenience, but to no avail. Her hormones dismissed it as an irrelevant technicality. This was her wedding night.

Her eyes seemed unnaturally bright, glittering with emotion and desire as she tried to work out what to wear. She turned and saw a package on her bed, a card in Elora's flowing handwriting.

'A small gift to commemorate the occasion.'

Opening it, Marisa gave a small gasp. It was a lehenga, but definitely not any old lehenga. This might as well have had 'hanky-panky' written all over it. The idea made her smile as she touched the sumptuously soft material, in her favourite red colour.

She changed quickly, carefully packing away the wedding sari, wondering if one day her own daughter would wear it at her wedding.

Would she encourage her daughter into a loveless marriage of convenience? She pushed the question away. Would Kieran allow that? Another issue she didn't want to think about. It wouldn't be up to Kieran to agree or disagree.

One last look at her reflection, one last calming breath and Marisa went downstairs, stopped on the threshold of the dining room and gave a small gasp. Surprise and appreciation combined. The room was illuminated with candlelight, the curtains closing out the sunlight so it could be any time of day rather than early evening.

Two places were set at the table and a warmth heated her as she saw what he'd done. Each place mat held a large banana leaf, laden with a selection of different dishes.

She turned as he entered the room, and her breath caught. He'd taken the time to have a shower, his blond hair slightly damp, with a hint of curl. Dressed simply in a shirt with the sleeves rolled up and chinos, he looked amazing. He stood in the doorway, his blue eyes rested on her with such obvious appreciation that she flushed, felt her skin shiver in response.

'I like the outfit,' he said. 'A lot.'

'Thank you, and thank you for this.' She gestured to the table, felt an incipient tear threaten. 'You've done the traditional wedding meal.'

'Yes. I know on Sarala there are forty-three dishes—I haven't managed that. But I did choose a selection of each type. I have sweet, salty and spicy. I made sure there were plenty of chillies and everything is pregnancy friendly. I loved the idea behind it. That marriage is made up of all those elements.'

'Our traditions and ceremonies show how seriously we still take marriage and I believe that is important.'

'So do I.' His voice was serious now and she wondered if he was thinking of his first marriage, entered into for different reasons. That had been a marriage of love. 'That's why the vows we took were important. They aren't just words. And all the different elements represented in this food tell us that a marriage isn't one-dimensional, it's about working together, complementing each other, balance.' He gave a sudden laugh. 'Anyway, enough philosophising. I have some alcohol-free champagne on ice as well as some freshly made lemonade. It's not the same as cocktails but...'

'Definitely better for the baby,' Marisa said and placed her hand on her tummy in an instinctively protective gesture. She looked up and frowned. Kieran seemed to have frozen, and he was staring at her as if he'd seen a ghost, his eyes shadowed. Then before she could do more than open her mouth he'd risen to his feet.

'I'll go and get the drinks.'

As he left the room, she told herself she must have imagined it: a trick of the light and shadows. Yet as the minutes ticked on, she wondered.

Kieran stood by the worktop, both hands clasped round the edge, and forced himself to focus on the counter, the smooth grey of the marble, the shine and sheen of its polished gloss, the flecks of darkness that patterned it. He hoped the mundane details would push down the memories triggered by Marisa's instinctive gesture. The image of Aisla performing the exact same movement, her slender hand resting on her tummy as she told him she was pregnant, her chin tilted in defiance, in challenge. Aisla's remedy to fix their marriage had been to have a baby. Would it have worked? Kieran didn't know. But he knew he would have tried. Knew whatever happened he would have loved the baby, his child, their child.

Now there was another child who needed his love, deserved his love, and this time he would not let his child down. He would be here for this baby, with every fibre of his being. And he would be here for Marisa as well, for the mother of his child. He would create a happy, secure place for their child to thrive.

He had meant what he said: he would make Marisa happy.

'Kieran?'

He heard her voice, soft with concern. 'Are you OK?'

'I'm fine.'

'No. I don't think you are.' Her voice was gentle but clear and now she was next to him, resting one hand on his arm. As he looked down at the swirl of the henna tattoos on her hand, the feel of her fingers sent a warmth running through him. 'And that's OK. Today… it's a massive thing. Getting married. And it's only a few days since I told you that you are going to be a father.' And again she touched her stomach and this time it didn't evoke any emotion except a further warmth. A further determination to get it right. 'It's definitely all right to have a moment.'

Now he turned, felt the counter press against him, and she turned too, so she faced him, looking up, and it seemed completely natural to bend down and kiss her. Natural and gloriously right. Her lips tasted of cherries, her hair that was now entwined round his finger was glossy and silken soft. He felt the sheer sweet jolt of need and yearning as she parted her lips and now he was kissing her properly and her arms were round his neck, her body pressed against his, and for a while there was nothing and no one in the world except for them.

Then, oh, so gently, she pulled away, stared up at him, her brown eyes wide with desire and need. 'Kieran?'

He placed a finger on her lips, pressed his forehead against hers.

'It's OK.' He gave a sudden smile. 'The night

is still young and it can go however you want it to. But now, let's eat and drink and celebrate.'

'I'd like that.' Reaching up, she cupped his cheek in one hand and then stepped back, with a sudden cheeky smile. 'And you're right. The night is still young. And I'm hungry.'

He followed her back to the table, aware of an unexpected sense of lightness, of anticipation, the air now suddenly seeming to shimmer with possibilities. He poured the sparkling amber liquid into both their glasses and held his up.

'To us.'

'To us,' she said and took a sip, before putting down her glass and picking up what looked like a crisp, but he knew it wasn't.

'That's a banana chip, right?'

'Yup. So instead of potatoes it's bananas, soaked in turmeric and cooked in coconut oil and salted. I think they go best with lime pickle.' She dipped one into one of the pickles and handed it to him. 'Try it.'

'That really is good. Jai assured me she had found an excellent caterer who would be able to make everything I wanted.'

'She definitely did.'

Kieran glanced round the table and picked up a piece of paper. 'She gave me a list of everything I chose; even wrote everything down for me. In the spirit of risk taking, I got jack-fruit crisps as well. And *inji thayir*. I know I'm not pronouncing that right, but I thought a ginger and yoghurt curry sounded interesting and of course I chose lots of chilli-based things.'

'It's perfect.'

'I'll tell Jai. She and Amit have been incredibly helpful. Even Amit telling Rohan worked out, I think?'

'Yes. I am glad Rohan and Elora were there today; but it will complicate things for him with my parents. They are already trying to come to terms with his decision.'

'Are they angry?'

Marisa hesitated, as if she was trying to find the right words. 'Not angry exactly…more bemused. They truly don't get it. To them Sarala is everything. I mean, they love us, their children, but Sarala is more important. They don't understand how he *can* step away; if I'm honest, I'm not sure I fully understand either, but I have always known in his heart he has never wanted to rule and I respect his courage in standing down.'

'But he wouldn't have done it if he didn't believe in you,' he said gently.

'Perhaps,' she said. 'But now I need my parents to believe in me.' She gave her head a small shake as if to banish doubts. 'I know nothing about your family. Your parents. Do you have siblings?'

'I'm an only child. My parents are great. Lovely people.' Guilt tapped him on the shoulder; when was the last time he'd seen his parents? Months and months ago—because he couldn't cope with their sympathy, or their grief. They'd been so excited about the prospect of becoming grandparents and they had been devasted for him after the accident, but all their sympathy did was make him feel worse because he knew he didn't deserve it. He didn't want to take the comfort on offer. And now… it was easier to have the occasional phone conversation or flying visit, where nothing but platitudes were spoken.

'They are both retired now. Mum was a solicitor and Dad was an accountant and I had a happy childhood. Very middle class, I suppose, but they encouraged me to try different things. Mum loved dancing. I think she wishes she'd become a dancer but she took the safe option. She took me to ballet classes and, oddly enough, I loved them.'

'Didn't people tease you?'

'No, because she also took me to martial arts. I loved doing both things. My dad is a football fan, so he used to take me to matches. I was never a good player but I supported his team and we used to go every few weeks every season.'

Something that had stopped after his marriage; he'd blamed work, but it hadn't only been that and, of course, his parents had known it. Aisla had never liked his parents, had resented time spent with them. And, filled with guilt that Aisla hadn't been happy, Kieran hadn't fought his parents' corner and his parents had never once said a word of censure or blame. 'My parents are very understanding, accepting people. They have always supported me.'

'Even when they don't agree with you?'

'Even then.'

She looked suddenly wistful. 'That must be lovely, that sense of unconditional love, the freedom to know you can express your opinions, ask for advice, but that's what it is. Advice, not instructions.'

'That's part of life,' he said. 'Making mistakes so you can learn from them.'

Marisa nodded. 'As long as you do learn,' she said. 'Your parents sound like good people. Have you told them about us?'

'I called them this morning; they have agreed that if they are contacted by the press they won't talk to them in detail, but they will say they are very happy about our marriage.'

Her face became troubled. 'I'm sorry—they

must be confused and of course they aren't happy. How can they be?'

'I told them this is what I want and actually they did sound happy for me. And when they find out about the baby they will be over the moon. They will love being grandparents; I hope you'll be happy for them to be involved.'

Marisa's face held genuine puzzlement. 'They are your parents, of course I would want them to be involved.'

'Good. Thank you.' He saw Marisa was still looking worried. 'I hadn't thought,' she said. 'I'm sorry. This all impacts so many people.'

'But it will work out. My parents will be all right about this.' Of course, they had reservations, but he knew once the baby was born, once they saw that this marriage would be one of contentment, they would see it was all for the best. He smiled at her, wanting to convey reassurance. 'It's all going to work out; we're going to build a solid marriage and provide our baby with a secure, happy, loving childhood.' He lifted his glass. 'To the three of us.'

'To the three of us,' she said, clinked her glass against his, then rose to her feet. 'Wait here. I'll be back.'

CHAPTER EIGHT

MARISA RE-ENTERED THE room a few minutes later, saw that Kieran had cleared the table in her absence and, suddenly nervous about what she was about to do, she paced over to the mantelpiece and remained there until he came back from the kitchen and joined her, one eyebrow lifted in query.

She looked up at him gravely, uncustomary shyness in her eyes.

'You look uncharacteristically indecisive,' he said.

'That's exactly how I feel. So, I'm just going to do this. I have a gift for you, but please don't feel you have to accept it. I will completely understand if it doesn't sit right and...'

Jeez, Marisa. Get on with it.

Abruptly she pulled her hand from the folds of her lehenga and handed him a long oblong jewellery box. 'It is traditional on Sarala for the bride to give her husband a gift, this particular gift in fact. Neither men nor women wear wedding rings here but this represents prosperity and happiness. I know that maybe you won't feel comfortable wearing it, but I wanted to do something for you to show you, to say thank you for today and for agreeing to this and coming up with a campaign and—'

'Marisa?'

'Yes.'

'You're clutching it very tightly. I think you should just give it to me. If that's what you want to do. But if you don't feel comfortable, then that's fine too.'

'Promise me you'll be honest.'

'I promise.'

He waited and Marisa realised she was *still* clutching the box and was now regretting the whole enterprise. This wasn't how this tradition was supposed to go. She was making a complete botch of the whole thing. Couldn't carry this off. Was making it even more awkward than it needed to be. Maybe it was a terrible idea. Or maybe she simply needed to let go of the box.

Abruptly she thrust the box out, not sure whether to watch him open it or not, but in the end she forced herself to look. He opened the box carefully, his large fingers so capable and dextrous and she felt a sudden flash of desire, so powerful that she blinked, clenched her hands. The only good thing was that desire at least temporarily dislodged her anxiety as he opened the box and looked at the contents.

'It's a chain,' she said, the words falling out in a burst, even as she knew she was stating the obvious. 'It's gold, interwoven with beads. Seven black beads that will protect the energies of our marriage and represent hope, and optimism. But I get you may not be a chain-wearing sort of guy.' She didn't even know that much about him.

'I want to wear it,' he said. 'I appreciate the thought and the tradition behind it.' He took the chain out and put it on in one sure movement, his blue eyes turned from her while he did so, and for a moment she wondered if he was wearing it for show, to be kind, to bolster the illusion, another prop for social media. Realised she had no way of knowing.

'Now,' he said, 'how about one more tradition?'

'What's that?'

'A dance. I know there's no one else here to watch us have the traditional first dance, but I don't mind if you don't.'

'I don't mind at all. Is jazz all right?' Even as she asked the question she wondered if that was the right choice, but suddenly she didn't care. She was tired of second-guessing and over-thinking. Trying to work out what was real and what wasn't.

'Jazz would be perfect.'

She put the record on, and the haunting notes streamed into the air, each one so evocative of times gone by, of emotion and feelings and beauty. Closing her eyes, she was transported back to their first date as she stepped into his arms, only tonight it was different. Back then she'd believed, they'd both believed, that all they had was one night. Now...this was their wedding night, the first day of their union, of a lifetime commitment.

And as his arms encircled her waist and she placed her hands on the muscular breadth of his shoulders there was no need for words. All that mattered was the music and the glorious sensation of being close to him, as one song merged into the next.

And then she looked up at him. 'You said earlier this night could be whatever I wanted it to be. Did you mean that?'

'Yes.' The word was simple and sincere. 'No pressure, we can just go with the flow.'

She nodded, stood on tiptoe and brushed her lips against his and heard his intake of breath, felt his instant reaction as he pulled her closer to him and then they were kissing, and this time she knew with absolute certainty that nothing was going to stop them. For one millisecond it occurred to her that perhaps they should talk about this but then sheer glorious sensations washed over her as he pulled her up in one effortless motion so he was carrying her, and the small voice was doused in the surge of need and desire. And then they were in her bedroom and he slid her down his body and looked down at her.

'What would you like to do now?' he asked and the deep rumble of his voice, the hint of laughter, anticipation and promise made her smile in response. Instinct took over as she reached for the buttons on his shirt, fumbling in her haste, tugging and pulling, frantic to see him, feel him, taste him.

And then she was lost in a glorious vortex of sensations.

It was hours later when Marisa opened her eyes, aware that something had awoken her. Her last memory was one of satiation, laughter, then drifting into exhausted sleep, her head on Kieran's chest. Now, though, she was on one side of the bed and she realised it was Kieran who had woken her up. He was clearly in the grip of a nightmare, his body moving in discomfort, and now he called out.

'Aisla. I'm sorry. Aisla. I'm so sorry...'

The words were heart-rending and Marisa froze. She had no idea what to do but she also knew that Kieran would not want her to be witnessing this. She was unsure if she should wake him up, unsure if that would be good for him, unsure if she could face seeing his guilt. Was he apologising for marrying Marisa, for having slept with her, for...betraying Aisla?

Before she could decide what to do, he shifted again and now he turned, tugged the blanket up and seemed to settle into a deeper sleep.

Marisa stared at the ceiling, the sensations of the past hours, that sense of connection tarnished now with reality. Kieran had lost his wife, a woman he'd loved and expected to spend the rest of his life with.

Marisa was nothing compared to that. She was just a woman he had married through duty and necessity. A woman he was creating an illusion with, a fantasy to sell to her parents and the public. And Marisa was mixing things up, mixing up attraction with emotion, mixing up illusion and reality.

Just like with Lakshan.

Lakshan had woven an illusion of love and togetherness, that rank and wealth didn't matter, that love could conquer all. An illusion that he loved her. And Marisa had believed it to be real, had been conned by a charlatan.

Kieran had been honest about the illusion. He was no conman. In this case Marisa was the one who wasn't able to separate fiction from fact. Who was once again letting physical attraction affect her judgement. And it had to stop. She had to face reality fair and square.

Oh, so carefully, she shifted further away from him, desperate not to wake him. She lay sleepless on the edge of the bed, her mind racing as she decided what to do, how to get control of events.

Kieran woke, aware that his head felt slightly heavy, aware too that something didn't feel right. Opening his eyes, he reorientated himself, realised at the same time what was wrong. The bed was empty, the place next to him cold to the touch, which meant Marisa had been up for a while. He glanced at his watch: seven a.m. Perhaps she'd got up to get ready for their meeting with her parents? Perhaps she couldn't sleep? Perhaps she regretted the previous night?

He climbed out of bed, used the bathroom, dressed and went to find his wife. Following the smell of coffee, he entered the kitchen.

Marisa was sitting at the kitchen table, dressed in a dark blue salwar kameez.

'Good morning,' he said.

'Good morning.'

He studied her smile, a smile that didn't reach her eyes, that held a certain wary remoteness.

'Coffee?' she asked 'And I can make some cheese and chilli toast.'

'Sure. That sounds good.' He kept his voice neutral, sensing she wanted him to keep his distance, though he wasn't sure why. He remembered the night before, how close they had been, how connected, moving together in such exquisite, perfect synchronicity, intuitively knowing what the other one wanted.

She rose and he sat down, thanked her for the coffee, shook his head to milk, realised the irony that they didn't even know how the other took their tea and coffee.

He remained silent as she made the breakfast, took a bite of the cheese toast and nodded his approval, enjoyed the spicy tang of the chillies and the slightly unfamiliar cheese melted onto a flatbread. Once they'd finished, he tried a smile. 'This was really good. Thank you.'

'You're welcome. It would be a good idea for you to pack after we've eaten.' Her words were stilted, formal almost. 'I'm not sure if we'll come back here after our meeting with my parents.'

'No problem.' He didn't have a lot to pack.

'But before you do that we need to talk. About last night.'

'Go ahead.'

'It was amazing.' She gave a small smile. 'A night to remember.'

'But?' Kieran wasn't sure what was coming, unable to read anything on her face except resolution and that sense of withdrawal.

'But you asked what I wanted and I've realised that while I don't regret last night, I don't think we should repeat it any time soon.'

A pang of hurt struck him, a sense of rejection that triggered a warning bell in the back of his mind. An alarm that things were getting complicated, personal, emotional. All the things he did not want in this marriage.

'Because there are more important things we should be focused on. Like this meeting with my parents. That's what we should have been thinking about last night. How to handle that; how to pursue our campaign. Does that make sense?'

'Yes. It does.' And it did; they couldn't let desire become so all-consuming. Because that *would* make things complicated, personal and emotional. This marriage was about their baby;

his focus should be on the baby, on being a good father, on safeguarding his child's future. 'You're right.'

And she was, and yet for a second he sensed that there was something else at play here, something he couldn't work out. But in the end that didn't matter. 'So, let's start now.' He glanced at his watch. 'Our meeting is in a few hours. So this is what I have gleaned about your parents—they are good and just rulers. I have researched their backgrounds and from what you have told me they are united in their love for the country and will always put Sarala first.'

'Correct.'

'OK, but what about them as people? When we go in today are they likely to get angry, to shout, or will they accept it and move on?'

'They won't make it personal; for them it is the effect on Sarala. They are already worried that I am seen as an out-of-touch princess because I have spent so much time abroad. Now I've married a foreigner. The Saralan people won't like that.'

'Why *did* you spend so much time abroad? I can see how much you love your country. Why leave it?'

There was a pause and when she answered he sensed the answer was rehearsed. 'I knew that I could never have an important role on Sarala, so I had a choice. I could stay here and become bitter or I could go to Europe and try and forge a different life for myself. That's what I did. Then Baluka became a republic and I knew I'd be needed here. So, I came straight back to Sarala. Soon after that Rohan abdicated and you know the rest.' He sensed there was more to it than that, but respected her right to privacy.

'Then we'll have to get your parents to see that, however much they don't approve of what you've done, we can make it work for Sarala. If we back each other up and show a united front, stick to the story, we can convince them.'

Marisa nodded. 'Sure,' she said, but he could hear the trepidation in her voice, knew that there were some undercurrents here he wasn't aware of. He knew too that he couldn't force her to tell him. Which meant he would have to wing it.

Marisa looked out of the window at the winding roads taking them towards the palace, anxiety twisting her insides with the knowledge that her parents were going to be disappointed in her. Again. First Lakshan, now Kieran. For her parents, it would be proof she hadn't learnt anything, hadn't changed from her eighteen-year-old self. And right now, that was exactly as she felt, the dread in the pit of her stomach escalating as they pulled up outside the palace and made their way to the throne room accompanied by an equerry.

'Her Royal Highness, Princess Marisa of Sarala,' he announced and turned to look at Kieran in question.

'Kieran Hamilton,' he said evenly.

The equerry made the announcement and then turned and after a formal bow he left, the door softly thudding shut behind him.

'Amma, Papa…' Marisa stepped forward and knelt, as tradition dictated.

'Marisa.' There was no smile on either parent's face but Marisa forced herself to rise and hold their gaze. She saw eyes that already held anticipated disappointment, and self-recrimination surged along with disappointment in herself.

'And your mystery guest,' her mother said, her voice tight. 'Kieran Hamilton.'

Marisa had no doubt that somewhere security was running a check on Kieran even as they spoke.

Silence loomed, and Marisa realised she had no idea what to say. All their planned words had flown from her mind as Kieran stepped forward and made the traditional sign of respect she'd taught him.

'I am pleased to meet you and I'd like to remove the mystery element. As you now know my name is Kieran Hamilton and yesterday your daughter did me the honour of marrying me.'

Marisa forced herself to remain upright, back ramrod straight. She moved a step closer to Kieran in an instinctive desire to protect him as she saw disbelief chase anger across her father's face, the expressions controlled but obvious to anyone who knew the King. A quick glance at her mother saw a depth of horror, shock and disappointment that cut Marisa to the very core, making her feel small, and insignificant.

'Married,' the Queen said, her voice full of disdain.

'Yes,' Kieran said.

But her mother did not so much as glance at him. Her gaze remained on Marisa and, unable to hold it, she looked down at her feet, aware now that Kieran had shifted closer to *her*, and that enabled her at least to look up as her mother spoke.

'So you have risked your position, risked

King Hanuman shrugged. 'But I would have gained something as well.'

'A son-in-law who would want power. I don't. I want to offer help and support.'

'Keep going.'

'I have done a lot of reading on Sarala and I know you have said you want to show that the monarchy is modernising. With us you have the the perfect way of showing you have moved with the times. If we sell this right, it will give Sarala something to celebrate. Things are tricky at the moment, an abdication, a female heir and no further heir. I also understand that the people wish to see a marriage—so here is an opportunity for celebration and festivities and positivity. After news of a republic and an heir standing down. The people want a marriage; this is a marriage. All we have to do is sell it as a good deal for them and for Sarala. Plus there will be no scandal, no forced marriage, way less prospect of a future scandal— Sarala wouldn't like to know their future ruler was forced to marry.'

'Is that a threat?' Queen Kaamini asked.

'No. This is me pointing out that I am better than the alternatives.'

It was, Marisa had to admit, a perfect answer, and she saw her father's lips quirk upwards ever so slightly in acknowledgement.

'So, you're saying make the best of it; it could be worse. And perhaps we could if you weren't already married. We can hardly get behind a wedding that has already taken place in a cloak-and-dagger manner.'

Now Marisa knew it was imperative she speak. She sensed her mother's eyes on her, knew that despite everything her mother loved her and her mother knew her and would be wondering at her silence. And her mother's intelligence, honed by that love and knowledge, might make her land on the truth, the real reason for a cloak-and-dagger marriage. And then…her disappointment in her daughter would hit a level that Marisa would never be able to recover from.

'Not cloak and dagger,' she managed. 'We married *privately*.'

'With Rohan and Elora in attendance,' Kieran supplied.

'Your brother knows of this.'

Marisa wanted to answer but the disapproval in her mother's voice, the knowledge that now Rohan was embroiled in this mess, rendered her silent. Again. So Kieran had to step in. Again.

'Yes,' he said firmly. 'He wanted to come with us today but we said no. Both Marisa and I wanted to tell you ourselves, because we stand by our actions and believe in this marriage. We kept it private because we were worried about your response, but also because we didn't feel it was fair for the taxpayer or you to foot the bill for lavish celebrations when there are already celebrations planned for Marisa's coronation as heir.

'But as a sign of my commitment to Sarala I would like to host a celebration, a party to celebrate our marriage. We can invite important Saralan figures and also offer attendance as a lottery to citizens from all walks of life. I will bear the cost.'

Marisa blinked, sensed Kieran was on a roll, knew the offer would help gain her father's acceptance if not approval. The King was a pragmatist.

'You cannot buy our support,' the Queen said quietly. 'Or the people's.'

'I know that. But I can at least not expect them to pay for a celebration they may not welcome.'

'We will accept this marriage,' King Hanuman said, heavily. 'But we do not like having our hands forced. I believe you mean well, Kieran, but, for all your words, for Sarala a marriage with a prince, an aristocrat, one who loves this country or understands the art of ruling would have been our preferred choice.

But it is done and for now I see no option but to put a brave face on it.'

'That is all we ask. That and that you give us, give me a chance to prove myself.'

Marisa could feel herself shrivel further inside, saw the resignation and weariness in her father, saw his aura dented. As for her mother, she could see the all too familiar frustration and regret and disapproval.

'That I grant,' her father said. 'We will announce the wedding. We will somehow impose some damage limitation on this event. In the meantime, it would be best if you made yourself scarce while we try to sort out the mess. Go to our royal beach place in Maraya for your honeymoon.'

Kieran opened his mouth as though to argue, before glancing at Marisa, who merely shrugged in acceptance. He'd done his best, but nothing could take away the fact she'd failed her parents. Again. She sensed her mother's eyes on her, tried and failed to hold the Queen's gaze, unable to look at the depths of disappointment there, made worse because it was tempered by love.

Images from the past crowded her mind. There were the same expressions on her parents' faces, the same heaviness of their voices. It had been ten years before and now it was all getting mixed up; the past and present, the same bleak, absolute knowledge that she'd let down her parents, her heritage, people who loved her and perhaps her very country itself weighted her tummy.

'We will go,' she said.

CHAPTER NINE

THE CAR MADE its way towards the royal beach house in Maraya, wherever that was, though its location was the least of Kieran's concerns. He glanced sideways at Marisa and noticed the way her hands twisted in her lap, the way she kept her gaze averted.

He glanced at the sliding soundproof panel that ensured their privacy from the chauffeur. 'Marisa?'

'Yes?' Her voice sounded low, uninterested.

'I know the meeting with your parents has upset you. But do you mind telling me what happened back there?'

'What do you mean?'

'I mean you barely said a word. What happened to backing me up, telling our story, selling ourselves?'

'I realised it didn't make any difference.' She shook her head. 'Don't get me wrong, you did a great job. But nothing you said or did can change the facts. No illusion can obscure the reality.'

'What reality?'

He saw the brightness of her eyes, knew she was holding back tears. 'I've screwed up. On all levels. I should never ever have gone on a date, not with you, not with anyone. Or I should have walked out of that restaurant and then we wouldn't be in this mess. None of this would have happened; I would have had a meeting with my parents today to discuss who I should marry, someone who would have been truly good for Sarala. There would have been no need for them to carry out damage control.'

Hurt flashed through him, but alongside that hurt was bewilderment: this was not the same woman he'd spoken to over the past days, the woman who had proposed to him.

'We've been through this. Our marriage *is* good for Sarala.'

'Only because I'm pregnant. My parents don't know that. They think I've made a foolish, selfish, emotional decision and nothing I do now can ever change that.'

'You could tell them the truth. About the baby. The true reason we're married.'

'That would be even worse. They would never understand how I let this happen, why I went on a pointless date in the first place, risked a pregnancy, then told you about the baby. They would have expected me to do what was best for Sarala.'

'At any cost, to you, to me, to the baby?'

'Yes.'

'And you?' he said and now he heard the edge to his voice. 'Do you regret your decisions?'

'I don't regret the baby. How can I? She is an innocent in all this and I will never regret my decision to keep her.'

'But you regret telling me, involving me. You do wish you were free to marry a prince or a lord or *whoever* would be an easy sell to the people.'

'It's not only about being an easy sell,' she flashed back. 'It's not all about a campaign. My parents had a point. Prince Erik would understand things that you can't. A thakur is already invested in Sarala, already loves this country. Those are facts.'

'So, you do regret telling me? Yes or no?'

Right now, it seemed clear that she did, that already, this early into their marriage, he'd let her down, just as he'd let Aisla down. Could he have handled the meeting with her parents better? If he'd listened more, listened better. Spent the previous night preparing as Marisa had said they should have. This was why the decision they had made that morning was correct. No more giving in to desire; from now on he would focus on doing right by his child, right by Marisa. There would be no more regrets.

She had taken time to gather her thoughts but now she spoke. 'Of course I believe a father has the right to know about his child. But in this case maybe there was a justification in not telling you. If I'd acted how my parents expected me to it may have been better for the baby, for me, for Sarala. Now they may well disinherit me; they will certainly never believe in me or my ability to rule.'

His own feelings dissipated at the anguish in her voice. 'They are your parents. You told me yourself that they love you. Surely, they won't judge you so harshly. Even if they think you have acted sentimentally, that is hardly a major lapse in judgement. You're only human. And I am surely not that bad a prospect?' Something wasn't making sense here.

'It's not about you. It's about me.'

'I think you should tell me what is going on,' he said. Seeing her hesitate, he decided to press the advantage, pushed the button that opened the panel separating them from the chauffeur and spoke. 'Could you pull over somewhere? The Princess would like some fresh air, so somewhere where we can have a pleasant, private walk.'

'Of course.'

Fifteen minutes later the car pulled to a smooth stop and, rolling down the window, Kieran saw they were on the edge of some woodlands. 'This is the Royal Forest of Urzu,' the chauffeur explained. 'Private land.'

'Perfect. Thank you.' He turned to Marisa. 'If you want to talk, you can, if not, you don't have to. But I don't believe there is any reason to regret our marriage.'

As they walked through the shade of the forest, Marisa inhaled the lush leafy smell of the vegetation, looked up at the massive height of the banyan trees that had been planned so many decades before and had witnessed so much Saralan history and no doubt heard so many conversations and confidences, arguments and inconsequential chatter, tears and laughter.

She turned to look at Kieran, and knew that he deserved an explanation.

'I'm sorry I left you high and dry in that meeting,' she said. 'And I am sorry that I am questioning everything, but it isn't your fault. I should never have believed that we would be able to pull this off, to sell this to my parents.'

'Why?'

It was a question she wasn't sure she wanted to answer but she knew she had to. She shouldn't have let him walk into that meeting without all the facts and now she'd hurt him, implied she regretted their marriage. A marriage that had been her idea. He had stood by her in that awful meeting, had defended her. The idea warmed her now, just as his reassuring bulk had warmed her then.

But it was a warmth that also engendered a sense of panic. It was all wrong. She should have been the one who took the lead; she should have been the one to speak their case. But she hadn't, all her words and thoughts had caught and tangled, all her self-assurance, any vestige of confidence had been dismantled by her parents' judgements. So, she had let him bear the whole brunt, relied on him, trusted him.

The idea was unwelcome—she needed to rely on herself alone; *she* was heir to Sarala and she wouldn't cede any of what came with that. But none of that was Kieran's fault.

She looked down at the ground, at the russet colour of the earth, the stray leaves and branches that littered the path, and then she began to speak.

'My parents and I have always had a complex relationship, especially my mother and I. I never conformed to what she believed a princess should be like, I was never the daughter she wanted or needed me to be. On Sarala in our culture the actions of the daughter reflect back onto the mother. If a daughter doesn't behave then it is deemed the mother's fault. And I didn't behave. Right from the start I wouldn't conform; I wasn't interested in pretty dresses or doing all the things a girl is traditionally taught to do. I never rated the fairy stories—I didn't want to marry the handsome prince. I wanted to sit on the throne.'

Kieran gave a small smile. 'I think that's fair enough.'

'Yes. But not here, not on Sarala. When Rohan was born, I was only two so it seems to me as though nearly my whole life everything felt unfair. Rohan got to be the handsome prince who got a happy ending and to rule a country. I was told I needed to learn how to be a good princess and one day I would get to marry for the good of my country. And for a long time, I didn't get it. Didn't get why it had to be like that; I was the eldest, why couldn't I rule?

'So, I was a "difficult" child. Once I cut all my hair off, a completely unacceptable action. I'd refuse to wear the proper clothes. In the end my mother told me if I truly wanted to rule Sarala I would love my country and I would conform to its traditions. I would show I could put my country first. She didn't explicitly say it, but I decided that meant if I showed how "good" I was I'd be given a chance to rule, that they would consider changing the law. So for a while I did conform and when I was eighteen, I asked them if, now that I had proved myself, they would make me heir.'

Marisa felt her face tinge with remembered embarrassment. 'They laughed; said they were sorry I had misunderstood but, surely, I must have known that wasn't possible. That they would never upend tradition like that. Worst of all they said if I truly loved Sarala, I wouldn't even have asked them to consider such an act. I was mortified.'

He reached out, took her hand in his. 'I'm sorry. That must have cut the ground from under your feet, made you feel small and angry.'

'It did, but that doesn't excuse what happened next. It was soon after all this happened that I met Lakshan. I was out, when I shouldn't have been out, walking, but not on palace grounds, and I bumped into him, or at least that's what I thought. He didn't seem to know who I was at first, but he offered to walk me home and he asked me out. To the movies. That's how it all started. He was very good-looking, full of charm, and I truly believed he didn't know my identity.

'Then one day he "recognised" me and he said that we had to stop seeing each other. But, of course, by then I'd fallen hook, line and sinker and I refused to give him up. As time went on I fell more and more under his spell. I was completely in his thrall. In the end he persuaded me to run away with him; he said we could get married, that he knew a pandit who would do the ceremony. He said once I'd spent the night with him my parents would be forced to accept the marriage.

'That should have made me pause but I was in love, couldn't bear the thought of losing him. He told me we were bound to be found out and my parents would stop us from seeing each other so this was the only way forward. He told me *he* couldn't bear to lose *me* and of course I agreed. He even got me to agree in writing. He said letters were romantic...' Marisa closed her eyes, could see her naïve, gullible younger self, pouring her heart out, words of love and passion. 'With hindsight it's all so obvious. He knew how to press every button, knew how to make me dance to his tune. All in the name of love.'

'Did you run off with him?'

Marisa shook his head. 'He never really intended to take things that far. Once I'd agreed he stopped responding to my messages. Then one day my parents called me to a meeting. In the throne room. They had my letters in front of them.'

She could remember her reaction. 'I thought they'd found out about us, had done something to him. I didn't even let them speak. I told them I didn't care what they thought. We were in love, that I'd agreed to marry him and I wasn't ashamed of that. That people's rank shouldn't matter... Lots of words to that effect.

'They let me say it all and then they told me Lakshan had given them the letters and was threatening to reveal them to the press and cause an immense scandal. It turned out he also had pictures of us in rather compromising positions. I was devastated. At first, I refused to believe them. I thought they were making it up. But it was all true. To make sure I believed them they brought Lakshan in; he confirmed it had all been a set-up, that he'd accepted a large sum of money and in return he was leaving Sarala, never to return.

'But what was almost as bad as my broken heart was the realisation of what I'd done, what I'd jeopardised. My reputation would never have survived the scandal; no one would ever have married me. And I knew how much I had disappointed my parents, how I had let them down. But I'd also proved them right—that I wasn't fit to rule Sarala, wasn't fit to do anything. They suggested I go abroad and I did. It felt like an exile but I felt I deserved it. I hoped I'd slowly regain at least their trust and maybe show them I could play some role in Sarala. I vowed I'd marry correctly, would do my duty as a princess.'

She came to a halt, suddenly exhausted, and Kieran looked round, found a tree stump and brushed it down.

'Sit down,' he suggested, and she nodded thanks, sat and he squatted down in front of her, took both her hands in his.

'So you see now why they are so upset—look at what I've done. Taken up with another unsuitable man, let my emotions overrule my judgement, put my feelings before the good of Sarala. I've demonstrated that I haven't learnt from my past mistakes.'

'Past mistake,' he corrected, his voice gentle. 'And an understandable mistake. You were the victim and you should have been given sympathy and understanding, not been punished with exile.' He shrugged. 'Perhaps a prince or a thakur would condone or understand your parents' actions but I don't. It's lucky for Lakshan that he left the country or I would find him and I'd drag him here to grovel to you on bended knees. You were a young woman, and you were taken advantage of by an unscrupulous conman. You did what so many teenagers have done before you: you made a mistake in love and it nearly took you too far.'

'Most teenagers aren't princesses.'

'I understand that as a princess you have a duty to your country, but royalty are still human. Part of being human is making mistakes and learning from them.'

'Exactly, and I clearly didn't learn from mine.'

'Because you went on a date? Because you slept with me? Because you fell pregnant by mistake? We used protection. You took no risks. Do you think you should have locked yourself up in a cage for the last ten years?'

Marisa stared at him, heard the outrage in his voice. 'Everything you say makes sense but it doesn't feel like that. I know I have let them down.'

Kieran frowned. 'If our child makes a mistake, do you want her to feel like this?' he asked quietly and the question shocked her, seemed to jolt her brain into another gear. 'Would you exile her?'

'Of course not.'

'Good. Because I won't stand back and let

that happen. I will never let my child feel she has let me down or disappointed me. I want her to be able to come to me, confide in me, discuss things with me. Like I did with my parents.'

Marisa felt a pounding in her ears. She knew Kieran was right, could suddenly see events from a different perspective. Of course, she would never want her child to feel like this, would never exile her, would never look on her with disappointment.

She rose to her feet, moved towards him. 'It's OK. You can stop. You're right. I get it.' She took a deep breath, reached up and gently cupped his face in her hands. 'Thank you. Thank you for being you, not a prince or a lord; for being you and putting things into perspective. And now I have a plan.'

'Go ahead.'

She'd dropped her hands and now he caught them in his.

'We get back in the car and we go back. Ten years ago, I let them send me off so they could clean up my mess. This time it's different. I'll clean it up myself. We'll go into the press conference with them, tell our story ourselves, show the people that we are a true couple, not to be hidden away and made excuses for. Show that as a family we stand together, that we believe in our marriage and believe it is good for Sarala.'

'Now that's a plan I can get behind,' he said with a grin. 'Let's go get them.'

As they walked back to the car, she pulled her phone out and called her mother, her heart beating fast.

'Amma. We're coming back. We want to be part of the press conference or, if you prefer, we will set up a separate one.' She knew this gave her mother no choice but to agree.

There was a silence at the other end and then her mother's voice came across. 'Very well.'

Once back in the car Marisa took a deep breath, turned to Kieran. 'So how do we do this? Any tips on how to sell myself?'

'Tell me about the people we are selling to.'

'They are people who truly believe that only a male can rule. My father had a delegation of business leaders in two days after the news of Rohan's abdication came in asking him to seriously reconsider letting me be heir, asking to speak to Rohan directly, citing concerns that the economy would tank with a female at the helm, that businesses would suffer, that people would no longer take Sarala seriously.'

'So very traditionalist.'

'Yes. But I suppose I could just about get my head around that. What shocked me more was that a separate group came to see my mother and these were women who had set up their own businesses and they also expressed their concerns.' Marisa let out a sigh. 'And I can't understand that. And I don't know how to sell myself to those women, because I feel as though they are betraying me.'

'Tell me about the women. Do the businesswomen of Sarala tend to have inherited a family business because they are the only child, and if so do they run the business or do their husbands?'

'It depends. Sometime they inherit but it is their husband who actually takes over. Or some do run a business, have set it up in their own right and aren't married or some are married and have supportive husbands.'

'Perhaps some of these women have worked out a way to keep their work life and home life balanced, perhaps for some it requires a lot of tact and diplomacy. Perhaps their husbands feel threatened by a female ruler. Perhaps for them it is a step too far. Ruling a country, upending such a massive tradition.'

Marisa looked thoughtful. 'A lot of the businesses consist of more traditional "women's skills". Making clothing, silk scarves, cooking. Perhaps these industries are more acceptable to the male ego.' She couldn't help the slight bitterness in her voice.

Kieran shook his head. 'Change takes time,' he said. 'Maybe years ago, it would have been impossible for a woman to run any business. Think of Ada Coleman, she was a pioneer over a hundred years ago and there has been a lot of progress since then, but it's been slow. I'm not saying it's right, but it is understandable. And if you go in all gung-ho, you won't achieve what you want. You can't drag people kicking and screaming to where you want them to be. You can't change everybody's mind, but you want some of them to choose to give you a chance.'

'Like you want people to choose your product.'

'Yes. But not everyone will and not everyone will like it. And sometimes it takes time to change people's attitudes. Sometimes you have to play a long game and show patience and understanding. Be persuasive.'

'Can you give me an example? A campaign you've run.'

'OK. Let's say you have two chocolate bars, they both have nuts, they are both milk chocolate and they both have raisins in them. Why would one person choose one over the other?'

'Mostly people may go for the better-known

brand, the one you associate with that choco-late bar.'

'Yup. So, jumping up and down going "mine is better", even if it is made with better quality nuts, isn't enough. You have to make people want to have better quality nuts.'

'How?'

'Well, the way we did it was kind of twofold. We tried to get nuts into people's heads. We played on words—who's got the bigger nuts? We also used squirrels. Had lots of people dressed up as squirrels offering people taste tests. And, of course, it's the packaging as well. That needs to be eye-catching. And it never hurts to make people smile. Don't rush. Use your words care-fully. Stick to the essence of the truth. And sometimes you have to compromise and some-times even that isn't possible.'

She thought she heard sadness in his voice but before she could even question it, the car pulled up outside the palace. Kieran reached out and took her hand in his. 'This is going to be fine,' he said. 'And even if it isn't it's better than running away and hiding.'

He was right and she wondered suddenly if that was what she'd been doing for the past ten years. Running and hiding. From her mis-takes, from her beliefs, from her convictions.

Well, now was the time to change things, to make a stand.

It was a sentiment she hung onto as she changed into an outfit she thought would project the right image, of a woman who respected tradition but was also willing to embrace change. A lehenga in the colours of the Saralan flag.

Right. That was that. She turned as Kieran entered, saw that he'd showered and by hook or by crook had got hold of a suit and that he wore it with a tie in the colour of the Saralan flag.

'Great minds,' he said with a smile. 'Now let's do this.'

And as they walked together into the press room at the palace, she felt him close to her, took reassurance and strength from his bulk, from his very presence. She focused on smiling for the cameras as she assessed the audience, who consisted of reporters from all conceivable publications, as well as some of the leading dignitaries and business leaders of the land.

She waited as her father spoke. 'Today our daughter came to tell us of an important and life-changing event.' A pause. 'Yet another one.' His words provoked a ripple of laughter. 'She has told us of her marriage.'

Now there was silence, followed by a hum

of conversation until King Hanuman raised his hand.

'We understand you must have many questions, indeed so did we. But to answer these questions in person, here is my daughter and her husband, Kieran Hamilton.'

Marisa hoped she controlled the small start of surprise; she'd expected her father to take the lead in this conference, but she got why he hadn't. She'd essentially rejected his offer to clean up her mess, so he would sit back now and see how she did.

Her heart beat faster as she realised how much was at stake. If she messed up here then her parents would seriously question her ability to rule, would question her judgement more than they already were. And they would be right to. They had given her this chance, a chance that she herself had asked for. Now it truly was down to her to prove that she could do this.

'Please go ahead,' she said to the audience.

'How long have you known each other?'

A relatively easy start, and she thought back to their illusory first date. 'We met at the beginning of November, a few months ago.'

'How did you meet?'

'Mutual friends thought we may hit it off, so they set up a date.'

'Why did you keep it a secret?'

'That's a fair question. Because we wanted to make sure it was real and we wanted to give ourselves a chance before we took on the pressures of going public.'

'How did he propose?'

Her mind went blank. Had they rehearsed this? No idea, but it wasn't something any woman in love would forget, and without skipping a beat she turned to Kieran. 'I'll let you field this one.' She gave a wide smile. 'I may cry, which would be embarrassing.'

That drew an appreciative sigh as everyone looked expectantly at Kieran. Who, to give him credit, didn't skip a beat either.

'I would love to sit here and say my proposal was a perfectly choreographed event, complete with champagne and violins. It wasn't. It was more…impromptu. A few months ago, our relationship was still very new and then suddenly Marisa's life changed—she learnt she was going to become heir to Sarala, a position she sees as an honour. It's a responsibility she is humbled by and will never ever take lightly.

'One day Marisa was coming round for dinner and while I was preparing it my phone beeped. It was a message from one of my friends, one of the people who had set us up in the first place. There was a link in it to an article, one that outlined possible husbands for Princess Marisa. Oddly enough, I didn't make the list.' This cued laughter.

'My blood ran cold at the very idea of Marisa marrying someone else, anyone else. I hated the idea of losing her. That's when I knew what I wanted, what I hoped she wanted too. I didn't have a lot of time to prepare. I couldn't even get a ring. But I did the best I could. I wanted to show her that I would embrace and respect Saralan traditions and cultures so I laid the table with a tablecloth the colours of the Saralan flag and—'

Marisa judged it was time to chip in. 'He made an Adhra chicken curry, which we all know is my favourite Saralan dish, and he'd even put extra chillies in it. And he made *nimbu pani* to go with it, proper lemonade, lime, roasted cumin, sugar and black pepper.' Nods of approval now. 'I have no idea how he managed it; he must have raced round the local supermarket while he looked up the recipes. The table looked beautiful, flowers, candles, and there was my favourite Saralan composer's music playing in the background. It was the most wonderful surprise and then with the dessert…'

'Which was, I have to admit, nothing more

exciting than chocolate ice cream…' Kieran added.

'He presented me with a formal written proposal… He was trying to work with one of our traditions, the *lagna patrika*. I know that is done as a family ritual, when the bride and groom prepare the formal invitation to the wedding with a date, but Kieran made it… personal.'

Marisa had no idea where this was coming from. Maybe it was because she knew this was the sort of thing Kieran would do, just as he had planned their wedding with such thought and care, the way he'd prepared their wedding dinner. 'And I said yes.'

'And in doing so your princess made me the happiest man in the world. I had no ring so instead I gave her a daisy chain, a necklace of flowers, and a promise to get a real piece of jewellery here on Sarala.'

Marisa nodded. 'But for me that necklace was the most thoughtful thing he could have done, a precursor to when we exchanged our flower garlands at our wedding just days ago.'

Which led into the next question. 'Where did you get married?'

Another relatively easy question for her to field.

But then, 'Why the secrecy? You married

without the consent of your parents. That is not traditional.' Before she could respond other questions were triggered.

'There are concerns about you being too westernised to rule—now you have married a Westerner in secret. How can anyone trust you?'

Panic threatened and she forced it down, managed a smile. Recalled Kieran's advice. Don't rush. Use your words carefully. Stick to the essence of the truth. That had all worked so far.

'That's a lot of questions,' she said. 'And they're all valid ones. We did marry privately, though my brother and his fiancée were present. We did that, without telling my parents, or Kieran's, because I didn't want the distraction of a large wedding, of all the plans and time that takes. Not when I want to focus on being Sarala's heir, on learning how to be worthy of the role, worthy of that honour, of your trust. I want that with all my heart.'

'But how is that possible?' The question came from Thakur Munshibari. 'You are a woman. In all of our history there has never been a woman ruler of Sarala. I do not question your heart; I question your ability to rule alone. We as leaders on Sarala had hoped to be able to stand behind you, but only if you had a man by your side, a husband who would be able to guide you. How can this man do that? He is a foreigner—he knows nothing of our ways. You yourself have been abroad too long.'

There were murmurs of agreement and the audience, who Marisa had felt to be veering towards her, were now being lost. She would not let that happen; that morning Kieran had defended her, now she would defend him. Would recall his advice, to keep calm, see other people's point of view, play the long game.

'I understand your point. Kieran does not know this country the way that you do, but he is willing to learn. He is a Westerner but in today's global world perhaps he can bring some new perspectives.' Now again she saw some people murmur in agreement, not all, but some.

Kieran leant forward. 'Marisa is right. I am more than willing to learn from all of you, and would deem it an honour if you would help me, give me some of your valuable time, show me your lands, or your businesses, teach me so I can support Marisa.'

Sudden doubts raced through her. Was this Kieran asserting a bid for power? Was he implying she needed guidance, that he would be the power on the throne and she would rule in name only? Marisa opened her mouth and then she thought, really thought.

Kieran had used the word support and wasn't that what this marriage was supposed to be about—being a partnership, an alliance? And right now, together, they were winning the room.

Kieran continued, 'My offer is made in all sincerity and of course I'd be happy for any press coverage of our visits as and when that is appropriate.'

Further nods at the idea of free publicity.

'I know I am a newcomer, but I would like the chance to earn your trust.'

'As would I,' Marisa said. 'I do truly understand your reservations. I understand that traditionally there has always been a male ruler of Sarala and I do truly respect tradition, our history and our culture. But I also want our island to move with the times, be part of the global world, show the world what a wonderful, amazing place Sarala is and how we can hold our heads high on a global stage. And my brother, Prince Rohan, believes in that too. He will work with me to promote our strong, beautiful island. I want to be a good ruler one day, many years in the future. In the meantime, I will try to learn to be worthy. All I ask for is some time and a chance to show you that I can do this.'

There was a pause and then the King spoke.

'I think what my daughter and her husband have requested are reasonable requests—time and a chance before a judgement is made. Marisa is my direct descendant and, while this is a break with tradition, I and Queen Kaamini are willing to grant time and a chance to this royal couple. Time before a decision is made. There is much to think about so we would appreciate now some privacy. We have offered the Maraya Royal Beach House to the newlyweds for a few days.'

'But we are happy to set up meetings and appointments for when we return,' Marisa concluded.

They waited while the press filed out and then Marisa turned to her parents. 'Thank you for the support.'

'It would have been foolish of me to not offer you time and a chance. Perhaps there will soon be an heir; that would set many minds at rest.'

'You should hope he is a boy,' the Queen said. 'It would make life easier.'

Marisa couldn't let that go. 'If we are lucky enough to have a baby all that matters is that the baby is healthy. Nothing is more important than that.'

To her surprise the Queen nodded. 'You are right.' She turned to Kieran. 'You did well; I will grant you that chance you asked for. And,

Marisa—it was a good decision to attend the conference. You acquitted yourself well there.' Then, perhaps having surprised herself by her own magnanimity, she rose. 'Perhaps now it would be best if you restart your journey to the beach.'

CHAPTER TEN

KIERAN GLANCED ACROSS at Marisa as the car traversed the roads taking them to their destination. He sensed she needed some space to process the day and he reached out and covered her hand with his. She turned to look at him and smiled, a smile so sweet, so uncomplicated, that something tugged in his chest.

'You OK?' he asked, his voice gruff.

'Yes,' she said. 'I am. Thanks to you. Even my mother showed approval.' He could hear disbelief and happiness in her voice.

'You were the one who faced that barrage of questions. You were the one under fire.'

'But I was only there because you showed me that I needed to stand up and be seen, not let my parents dictate events, clear up my "mess".'

'Then let's share the credit. And agree with your mother's verdict that we acquitted ourselves well.' He squeezed her hand gently. 'But it's not over yet. Now we need to win good opinion from the people. The real people. We need to be more visible, not just to the "important" people, but to the real people because, at the end of the day, they count. They are the ones whose lives you want to make better. They need to get to know you.'

'So, it's the next stage of our campaign? Another illusion?'

'No. This is real. You really want to be in touch with real Saralans and I am genuinely interested in getting to know the country I will be living in, the country our child will one day rule. But yes, it is also part of our campaign to win people over to accepting a female heir and accepting me. So, we need to sell ourselves and the idea of a romantic happy-ever-after ending.'

The idea should fill him with unease and yet it didn't. Somehow right now the illusion seemed one that would be easy to portray, a pretence that they could carry off with minimal effort. It must be the buzz of adrenalin, the knowledge that their campaign had scored a victory that day. Nothing to do with the fact her hand was still in his, nothing to do with her smile, with the look of concentration on her face.

'You're right,' she said. 'And I think we should start now. There's a village fair, local to the royal residence we're headed to. Let's go there. Now.' Her face lit with enthusiasm and determination and when he nodded, she pressed the intercom button and instructed the driver where to stop, and twenty minutes later they alighted from the car.

Kieran breathed in deeply as they entered a large field, feeling a sudden strange sense of new beginnings as he inhaled all the unfamiliar scents. The sweet smell of lush blooms intermixed with the tantalising smell of spices, the hot tang of chilli and the smell of smoke. He took in the sound of music, the beat of drums and the sound of pipes and a surge of something precariously close to happiness touched him.

'Lead the way,' he said, holding out his hand. And then she was right next to him, so close her shoulder brushed against him, her scent assailed his nostrils and, when she took his hand, a jolt of awareness rippled across his skin, and suddenly it no longer felt problematic to simulate being a couple. A real couple. Because it was easy...*too* easy.

But it also *wasn't* real; he mustn't forget that. While doing the right thing, it was right to try to make Marisa happy. To provide their baby with a happy home. The chance he'd never had with Aisla. Aisla. The baby, that baby. Gently, he put the grief away. He would never dodge his culpability but the here and now was about Marisa.

Marisa, who looked up at him with a beaming smile. 'I came here as a child a couple of times with my parents so I was on my best behaviour. But one year Rohan and I were staying up here with our ayah and she and a few staff members took us and we loved it. They shouldn't have done it really, but somehow Rohan and I persuaded them and it was magical. There were food stalls and dancing and we felt just like normal children.'

'So, you and Rohan were close.'

Marisa considered the statement. 'Yes and no. We get on, I would always have his back and vice versa, but maybe...' and now she sounded sad '...maybe I let resentment factor through a little bit, or maybe the knowledge of him being heir when I always knew his heart wasn't in it made a barrier between us. Because it wasn't something we could really talk about. We were so attuned to doing our duty, so sure that nothing could change the facts that there was no point talking about it. I hope, now that he is happy with Elora and free to follow his heart, that maybe we can rethink our relationship.'

'You will,' he said. 'I spoke with Rohan the

day of our wedding and his plans to promote Sarala are fabulous. Perhaps there are projects you and he could co-manage and I'd be happy to throw my knowledge into the ring to help.'

She looked at him. 'You have helped enough. I can see exactly why you are so good at what you do.' She hesitated. 'Now, enough about me. Everything has been about me and now I'd like it to be a bit about you.'

Her voice was way too serious, plus he didn't want it to be about him. He wanted it to be about her and as she looked up at him, the last rays of the sun dappled her hair, lit the strength and beauty of her face, the length of her dark lashes, the straight bridge of her nose, the gloss of her lips, lips that he knew the texture of, the taste of… And suddenly he didn't care about the intentions of the morning, the common-sense approach that said they needed to ignore attraction.

So he grinned at her. 'Everything hasn't been about you,' he said, aware that his voice had deepened, and her eyes widened as he wiggled his eyebrows. 'I can remember a couple of things last night that were all about me.'

It took a moment for the penny to drop and then she blushed, before narrowing her eyes. 'That was my pleasure,' she returned, and now the atmosphere ratcheted up another notch as images of the previous night streamed through his mind. The speed at which desire had elevated took his breath away. Because now all he wanted to do was kiss her, all he wanted to do in fact was return to the car and drive at top speed to wherever this royal honeymoon house was.

But they couldn't, and he saw that same realisation dawn in her brown eyes as she stepped back.

'This is exactly what we were talking about this morning,' she said and he nodded in acknowledgement.

They were letting attraction distract them from the matter at hand. They were here to become more visible, for him to learn more about the real Sarala. 'You're right,' he said. 'But that doesn't mean we still can't have fun. Just of a different sort.'

She smiled. 'Thank you for getting it. Let's go and do exactly that.' But as she took his hand and they started walking she looked up at him. 'So back to talking about you,' she said. 'I wanted to ask you about work. Your work. I know you said you were on a sabbatical, but at some point, you will want to go back, and I understand that. I don't want you to think that I expect you to remain on Sarala and only work for the good of my country. You have your own life as well.'

Kieran nearly slammed to a stop. His own life—he hadn't had that, hadn't wanted that. He had simply been existing in his project house in Scotland, focused on physical work. Now... now for days he'd been focused on something else, on helping Marisa and his child, in creating a campaign different from anything he'd done before and his brain had become creative again. And he wasn't sure how that made him feel.

'Yes,' was all he could think of to say.

'You don't sound very sure,' she said softly. 'But, for what it's worth, you are clearly so good at your job and you should probably reassure your partners that you are coming back. I mean, you can probably conduct some work from here? I don't want to hold you back. How long was your sabbatical for?'

Kieran took a moment and looked around, his gaze skimming the wares displayed on the row of stalls set up by the side of the field. Brightly coloured silk scarves, earthenware pots and plates, an array of fruit and vegetables, gleaming purple aubergines, luscious orange mangos and strings of glossy red and green chillies.

'Sorry. I didn't mean to pry.' Her voice was

small and he knew the silence had stretched too long.

'You aren't,' he said. There were things Marisa needed to know, would be expected to know. Questions that would come up in future interviews. But it was more than that: he wanted to tell her. The idea was strange, unfamiliar.

'I don't know. The sabbatical—it was more of a desertion. My creativity disappeared one day. I'm sure it wasn't instant but that's how it felt. After Aisla died, I threw myself into work, because it was the best way to cope. And I couldn't let Mark and Lucy down. When she died, we were on the brink of success—if I'd left then it wouldn't have been fair on them. Plus, work grounded me. And we did succeed; and then we needed to consolidate and we did and one day I realised we'd made it. Money and clients were rolling in, Mark and Lucy had got together, got married... And...it didn't seem fair. Or right. Here was the lifestyle I'd promised Aisla and she wasn't there to see it. So, I decided that was the time I could walk away. Lucy and Mark could easily keep the company on track. We'd hired some excellent staff. So, I changed tack. Went to Scotland, found a project house and I threw myself into working on that.'

'Tell me about the house,' she said.

It wasn't the question he'd expected but he welcomed it, sensed she knew how hard it would have been for him to speak of Aisla.

'It was a falling-down old mausoleum really, but it was a project that was physically demanding and required a completely new skill set of me. It felt like what I needed. It's still not finished but I was making good progress. I learnt how to build walls—I mean, I had help, but I worked alongside the builders. I learnt carpentry and I am doing as much as possible myself.'

'That sounds incredible—and to watch something transform from day to day and know you've achieved it must be incredibly fulfilling.'

The words surprised him. 'I'd never really thought of it like that.'

'Can I see pictures? We could sit, get some food from the stalls and listen to the music while you show me.'

'Sure. I do have some pictures. Not a lot but some.'

Ten minutes later they were sitting at a rickety wooden table, a selection of food in front of them, steam rising and sending a tang of spice and heat that tingled his taste buds with anticipation. 'This all looks amazing and smells even better, but I have to plead ignorance as to what a lot of it actually is.'

'This is one of my favourite dishes ever. *Kozhi porichathu.* Basically, it's fried chicken and I think every vendor makes it slightly differently.'

Kieran took a bite, savoured the explosion of taste, the hit of chillies, the mix of spices. 'Coriander?' he hazarded. 'Ginger…'

'Yup. I have to admit I'm not great at cooking, just eating, but Elora loves cooking; she could be a professional chef. She is actually researching a book on Saralan street food and, according to her, the chicken is marinaded first in a special chilli and ginger paste and then it's fried, and then it's tossed in a sauce made of tomatoes, green chillies, curry leaves and any other spice you like—I think Elora said cumin.'

'Amazing.'

'Then these are *dosas*, like a kind of pancake made with dal. This one is served with chilli chutney. Then I also got *gole bhaje*, they are a deep-fried batter made with fermented buttermilk so I won't have those but I promise you'll love them. And finally, I got *aloo bhonda*, which are essentially fried mashed-potato balls and they are incredible.'

'Excellent choices—I can tell that one of the things I'll like about living here is the food.'

He saw her small frown, wondered what she was thinking. 'So, what sort of food did you eat while renovating a house? What's your favourite food?'

Kieran tried to think. 'Nothing very inspiring,' he admitted. Food had seemed a bit like simply something that had to be done. 'There wasn't really a working kitchen so I did a lot of camping food, baked beans on toast, fry-ups, and quite a lot of cereal. Or I'd stop and get a bacon butty or a burger, which is not the same as street food here.'

'So, is there a kitchen now? Do you want to show me those photos now?'

He pulled his phone out, found the pictures and she shifted closer to him and he caught his breath, her proximity taking him unawares and instantly triggering the very attraction they had decided to hold at bay. For reasons that were all still valid. Perhaps even more so now that something had shifted, that creeping sense of happiness he'd felt, the way she'd confided in him and the anger he'd felt on her behalf...all combining to make him feel more alive than he had for a long time.

Alive.

An awareness of every sensation, every

spice—even food had taken on new meaning, new life.

Life.

An awareness now of how close she was as she studied the pictures, a tendril of her hair tickling his cheek, the scent of her shampoo.

And now darkness was beginning to close in, and people were lighting fires to illuminate the area.

'You've done an incredible job,' she said now, looking up from her intent perusal of the photos. 'You're making it into a beautiful home. I love the curved walls and the stained-glass windows are amazing. And the staircase. It's an amazing work in progress, a real transformation.'

As she spoke he seemed to look on the project with different eyes. For him it had been a means to an end, a way of achieving exhaustion through physical labour. But as he looked at the pictures, heard her words, he did feel a sense of pride in his achievement.

'It looks like your creativity rechannelled itself into this.'

And just like that the guilt came back and, as if she sensed it, she shook her head. 'I know you don't like to talk about it, but I believe Aisla would have been happy for your success— happy that you achieved all those goals and ambitions that she must have been part of. I'm sorry she didn't get to see that you succeeded, but I know she would have believed in you and she'd be happy for you. And proud. So, I understand why you took the sabbatical but I don't think she would have wanted you to give up your dream. And it sounds as though the company was your dream.'

Kieran looked at her, saw the sincerity in her eyes, heard the sympathy in her voice and knew he should repudiate it. Because Marisa had it all wrong. Aisla hadn't believed in his dream, hadn't wanted him to pursue it, had thought it was nothing more than a pipe dream. She'd thought that he was wasting time and money on a project doomed to ignominious failure.

But how could he tell Marisa that, without sounding as though he was criticising a woman who'd tragically died? How could he tell Marisa what he'd never told anyone, that his marriage wasn't a success, that he hadn't known how to make it one, that his pursuit of his dream was in fact selfish?

To do that would be to belittle Aisla's memory and he couldn't bring himself to do that, but to accept Marisa's sympathy felt equally wrong. Worse perhaps. Because he now also felt a sudden seeping fear that he'd mess up again, when now there was so very much at stake: this woman's happiness, a baby, a country, a birthright, a crown.

A sudden cry, a gasp, interrupted his thoughts.

He looked up and saw a group of people glancing over to them, looking down at their phones and gesturing.

'I think we've been recognised,' Marisa said.

'That's all right,' he said, the distraction welcome.

Marisa smiled as one of the group approached tentatively. 'Are you... Princess Marisa?'

'Yes, and this is my husband, Kieran. We're on our way to Maraya and we stopped at the festival because I wanted Kieran to sample some of our wonderful food and see how we celebrate.'

'Can we take a picture?'

'Of course.'

Several pictures later and Marisa asked the group, 'Are you going to join in the dancing? I remember when I was a child I loved how everyone of all ages joined in when the performers started.'

'Definitely. Are you going to dance today?'

Marisa hesitated, glanced at Kieran. 'What do you think?'

'I'd love to watch you all in action,' he said.

'And then you'll join in?' she asked, and now

a mischievous smile lit her face. 'I know you know how to dance.' She rose to her feet and held out her hand and together they headed towards the area where the dancers had just begun their performance.

Kieran watched, entranced. Each dancer had their hair pulled up in a bun atop their heads, each knot of hair encircled by a garland of white flowers. Their costumes dazzled the eye, brightly coloured saris, vibrant reds, oranges and yellows that all flowed together in a surge of colour, helped by their unique style— pleats formed a fan at the front allowing the leg movements to create cascades of flashing fabric. The ends of the sari were tightly pulled over the shoulder and then secured at the waist with jewelled belts, the gemstones glinting in the lights of the fire that flamed from the fire pits that surrounded the makeshift stage.

'It's a dance to celebrate the festival and the local deities, to give thanks for the harvest,' Marisa said. 'The patterns hennaed on their hands and feet represent the story.'

'It's beautiful,' he said quietly. They stood close together, hand in hand, no need for further words as they both watched, mesmerised by the dancers' grace, the perfect timing and synchronicity of their moves.

At the end the performers melted away, but

the music kept going and soon the spectators surged towards the stage and the surrounding area and began to dance, individually and in small groups, and with a backwards smile Marisa went with them.

Now he couldn't take his eyes off her as she lost herself in the pulsating beat of the music and somehow all the other dancers faded away and there was only her. His beautiful wife. Her arms, legs, her whole body moved with a sinuous grace, every movement telling a story, conveying an emotion, her facial expression matching the dance, the whole as much a measure of acting as dancing. So many emotions conveyed; love, sadness, laughter, all somehow communicated by the tilt of Marisa's head, her fluid movements.

And then she beckoned to him, the movement, her expression, the tilt of her neck, everything casting allure and temptation, and without even thinking he moved towards her, drawn like a moth to a flame.

Somehow as he drew near his body listened to the beat of the music, his mind worked out the base rhythm and movements. He found the best way to mirror and answer the story Marisa was telling, his whole being caught up in the music, and the connection the dance created between them. His emotions tumulted, he felt the tug of frustrated desire as she moved backwards, her finger shaking, and he stepped forward, arms and shoulders moving in pursuit. The performance was so tantalising, so teasing, his breath caught and his gut twisted with a yearning for her, a need to touch her.

Then the spell broke as the music came to a halt and he realised he and Marisa were now encircled by a crowd of people who all started applauding. He saw too how many people were taking photos and videos, the sight somehow forging a path of reality through the mists of desire, the thrall of the story of the dance.

'Again,' called someone and Marisa blinked, clearly as wrapped up in the moment as he had been.

Then she smiled but shook her head. 'I'm too tired,' she said and he knew that she was also thinking of the baby and wouldn't want to overdo it. 'But I absolutely loved that and I am enjoying every minute of our time here.'

There were good-natured nods and after a few more photos they managed to discreetly melt away, back into the throng of visitors, and soon were wandering through the field, when Marisa pointed. 'Fireworks,' she said.

They stood, anonymous now in the mass of spectators, and looked up at the sky and he was reminded of their imaginary first date, the

illusion becoming reality as they watched the
pop and sparks light the night sky. Then, instead of watching the colours light up the sky,
he turned to study the woman next to him, her
cheeks still faintly pink from the dance, her
hair freed now from its ponytail, cascading to
her shoulders in a riot of curls.

As if sensing his gaze, she turned to look
up at him and suddenly it seemed inevitable.
It was impossible not to turn to face her and
then they were kissing, a slow sweet kiss, one
almost without expectation, in the knowledge
now that they were in a public place and that
this could lead nowhere. And yet it felt significant, a kiss that marked an occasion even if he
wasn't sure what it was. A new beginning...
The thought was tentative but he allowed it in,
even if he didn't dwell on it.

They pulled apart as a gasp from the audience indicated the fireworks were approach-
ing the finale and, arms wrapped round each
other's waists, they watched the spectacular
bursts of colour that ricocheted and tumbled
through the sky.

'Time to go?'

Marisa nodded and they made their way back
to the car.

CHAPTER ELEVEN

FIFTEEN MINUTES LATER they arrived at a gated estate, surrounded by a bright white wall fitted with lights that turned on as they approached. They alighted and Marisa saw Kieran look up at the large, square, two-storeyed beach house. The top floor was encircled by a wide balcony, and the whole building was dwarfed by tall, skinny-trunked palm trees, their wide green-fronded tops shaking gently in the night breeze. He inhaled deeply, and so did she, took in the salty tang of the sea.

'The rear looks out onto a private stretch of beach,' Marisa said, before turning to the driver, who stood by the car. 'Thank you, Suvas. You can go home now. We will call you when we need you again. Thank you for today.'

The driver smiled and nodded at them both and soon he had driven off. 'There are no live-in staff,' she said. 'But there are local people who keep an eye on the place and prepare it for visits, so it will be clean. There is a house-keeper who has worked for us for decades, Amina, and I am sure she will come tomorrow to make sure we are happy with everything. But for now, it's just us.'

Just us. Marisa looked at him and her lips seemed to tingle in memory of their kiss, a kiss that still resonated through her whole body. It had awakened a tug of desire but also generated a sense of fuzzy warmth that still seemed to blanket her.

In some ways the whole day had generated that; she'd genuinely felt he had her back in a way no one had ever done before. He'd stood by her side, and now she allowed herself a soupçon of hope that maybe...

Maybe what, Marisa? Maybe nothing.

That way lay danger; she must not start weaving a rosy imaginary future. She was the Princess whose happy ending was the throne.

And yet...

She shook her head.

'Let's go in. I'll show you around.' But as she walked forward, she swayed suddenly and in an instant his arm was round her, steadying her.

'Not today,' he said firmly. 'Right now, you are going inside and you are going straight to bed. You must be utterly exhausted and you and the baby need a good night's sleep.' She opened her mouth to protest and he shook his head. 'No arguments.'

He was right; there was no denying the wave of exhaustion that overcame her. 'But—'

He shook his head. 'No buts either.'

She opened the front door, smelt the scent of polish and something floral, took a quick glance round the light blue walls of the hallway, and then, almost in a dream, led the way upstairs, and tried to figure out where to sleep. How would it work?

Kieran pushed open a couple of doors and then shepherded her into one of them. A room she'd once shared with Rohan, but now the bunkbeds had been replaced by two twin beds, the walls repainted, the whole place completely unfamiliar, but Marisa was so tired she didn't care.

'This will do,' Kieran said and swiftly swung her overnight bag onto one of the beds.

'You get ready. I'll go and get you a glass of water, unless you'd prefer a cup of tea or...'

'Water is fine. Thank you. But what about you?'

'Don't worry about me,' he said. 'I'll sleep in the other twin bed a bit later and we'll work everything out in the morning.'

Once he'd gone Marisa made herself find

her wash bag, made her way to the en-suite bathroom, brushed her teeth and then headed back to the bed, changed and snuggled down under the blanket, sure she'd stay awake until Kieran's return, even as her eyes closed. Somewhere at the point of being nearly asleep she was sure he came in, laid a hand on her head and brushed the lightest of kisses against her cheek, engendering a sense of warmth and security as she slipped into dreamless slumber.

A slumber that continued until the morning when she opened her eyes, instantly awake and aware of a sense of refreshment. Glancing over to the other bed, she saw it was empty, though a little rumpled, so presumably Kieràn must have slept there.

She climbed out of bed, used the bathroom and changed into a simple long floral summer dress and headed for the stairs. She paused as she heard voices from the kitchen, the deep rumble of Kieran's voice and a female voice in answer. Amina must have arrived early; Marisa composed herself, aware that the illusion needed to start from here, and yet there was no sense of nerves or anxiety, just a sense of leftover warmth from the previous evening.

She entered the kitchen and Amina turned. 'Your Highness.'

'Amina, don't be silly. You call me Marisa...

you know that.' Moving forward, she embraced the older woman in a hug. 'It is good to see you.'

'It is good to see you as well and to meet your husband.' The housekeeper looked at Kieran with what looked like approval.

'I have been telling Amina how late we arrived, how exhausted you were and that I tucked you up in what she tells me was once your and Rohan's room so you could sleep properly.'

'My daughter showed me the video of you and Kieran dancing—I am not surprised you are so tired,' Amina said. 'So today we have agreed that you will spend the day on the beach. and I will make a picnic. There will be enough food to last you all day. While I do that you can show Kieran around the house.' She made shooing movements with her hands and, turning away, headed purposefully towards the fridge.

Marisa nodded to Kieran and he followed her out of the kitchen.

'What happened?' she asked, once they were out of earshot.

'I heard the front door open and I guessed it was Amina. Luckily, I was already up so I went to waylay her, explained why we were sleeping in a twin room. She's a lovely lady and she's clearly fond of you. She gave me a bit of a lecture on how you deserve a relaxing honeymoon and came up with her beach-day idea, which I'm good with.'

'Me too. It's been a tiring few days.' And truth be told her heart did a funny little hop, skip and a jump at the idea of a day spent with Kieran. With her husband. On their honeymoon. *Careful.* 'It'll be good to relax and use the time to find out a bit more about each other. For next week and the interviews.'

'Sure. Good idea.'

'This is the living room,' she said, showing him the spacious lounge area, furnished with large comfortable sofas and chairs. She then led him to the vast double glass doors that framed a view of the sea, the stretch of aquamarine blue completely calm, spread like an immense blanket as far as the eye could see, edged with a line of pristine golden sand. 'Then there are two bedrooms down here and a bathroom. Upstairs is the twin room and the master bedroom. Now, I'm starving. Let's see what Amina has got ready for us.'

Half an hour later, holding a bag each, they headed from the back door and walked the short distance to the beach. Marisa glanced up at the sky and pointed to the rock face about a five-minute walk away. 'We can get some shade.'

Once there she opened her bag, took the stainless-steel tiffin out, and carefully unscrewed each lid, grinning as she saw the contents. 'The perfect Saralan breakfast. And Amina has even written out the ingredients so that I can explain everything to you.' She pointed to the top layer. 'That's sweet *Pongal*. I suppose it's a bit like porridge, or at least it looks a bit like porridge and has a similar texture. But it's made with yellow lentils and rice and a cane-like sugar called jaggery, then it's sprinkled with cashew nuts and raisins. And Amina has made something savoury too, *medu vada*, which are savoury doughnuts made with black lentils and served with a spicy sauce, called *sambar*, and a coconut chutney.'

A sudden qualm struck her; he'd agreed to give up so much without so much as mentioning it and now she was expecting him to love a whole new cuisine as well. 'I'm sorry—I promise it won't all be about typical Saralan cuisine. I will make sure we have a variety of food. I like European breakfasts, croissants and meats and cheese, and I am quite partial to a proper bacon butty myself. As long as the bacon is crispy.'

'Definitely. Crispy bacon is a must and the

right amount of condiments. I like a hint of mustard.' He looked at her. 'But don't look so worried. I am truly enjoying all this food.'

They started to eat and the familiar taste of Amina's food brought back a set of childhood memories. 'It tastes just the same,' she said. 'I can even picture Amina in the kitchen, making the *sambar*, mixing the ingredients.' The coriander seeds, the roasted chillies, the fenugreek seeds. 'Frying the doughnuts.' The smell of melted ghee mingling with the sizzle and aroma of the cooking spices.

'There are some foods like that,' he agreed. 'I remember having my best mate round and my mum would make sausages and mashed potatoes and her special gravy. Or spaghetti bolognese.'

'Then we'll make sure our child gets that growing up too. Your family recipes as well as mine.'

'I'd like that. Dad can make a pretty good Sunday roast too.'

'We'll make sure we visit the UK regularly and your parents are always welcome here. I was thinking…would you like to invite your parents here for a visit soon? They could stay with us. Once we decide where we will live. Or if they would prefer some privacy, we can find them somewhere to stay or perhaps a combination of both?'

'You'd have them stay with us?' She caught the surprise in his voice.

'If you were happy with that. Of course. They are your parents, our child's grandparents. That is incredibly important. They are family.' She frowned, seeing he still looked almost unsure. 'Don't you agree?'

'Totally. I guess I hadn't thought that you would want that.'

'Why not?'

He glanced away and then down at his empty plate and she thought she knew the reason for his hesitation.

'Do they not want to meet me? I know you said they would be all right about our marriage, but they must be a bit shocked and I'd get it if they aren't happy. But I'll try, I really will, to make them feel welcome and persuade them that this is a good idea.'

But even as she said the words she realised how hollow they were. Why would Kieran's parents welcome this: their son moving to a different continent, leaving them, leaving his whole life behind? Why had Kieran himself agreed to it so readily? She thought about the house he had put so much of himself into, left unfinished. There must be so many other things, things she didn't even know about. She pushed the thoughts away; Kieran had agreed and this was a day for happiness, not doubts.

'And you said they will love being grand-parents, so even if they won't come and see us now, maybe they will when we tell them about the baby?'

Kieran raised a hand. 'It's OK, Marisa. I think they would love to come and meet you.'

'Then why did you sound reluctant?'

'I wasn't reluctant, more surprised, I guess.' Another hesitation. 'Aisla didn't really get on with my parents. She felt that they disliked her, even though they didn't, and it made things a bit…complicated.' He made a quick gesture with his hands. 'It wasn't my parents' fault. They are lovely people… It wasn't anyone's fault,' he added hurriedly. 'But I suppose I was seeing parallels.'

She sensed his discomfort at speaking about Aisla, but a warmth touched her that he had, along with a need to reassure him. 'Relation-ships can be complicated,' she said softly. 'If your parents have doubts about me, about our marriage, I understand that and I promise I will do everything I can to overcome those doubts. But I will also do my best to make sure we get on. Everything you have said about them so far shows me that they are good parents and they love you. And I want my child to be close to their grandparents—my grandparents were a real influence in my life and I still miss them. So yes, they are welcome here, even if they are unsure about me.'

'Thank you.' Reaching out, he briefly covered her hand with his. 'I know they will like you.' He rose to his feet. 'Now, how about we go for a paddle?'

As they walked towards the sea and Kieran gazed out at the rippling azure water, he felt a strange sense of the tides shifting, a sense of promise, of an actual real future taking shape. A future with a child, a little girl with Marisa's curly dark hair, sitting at a table eating sausages and mash with *sambar* sauce as gravy. An image of himself and Marisa telling their daughter stories, of his parents being part of his life again. His life, his future…the idea felt possible in a way he wouldn't have imagined just weeks before.

'Is it safe to swim here?' he asked as they sat at the edge of the water, inhaled the briny scent, listened to the splish-splash of the lapping waves.

'Yes, the currents are fine and Rohan and my dad used to go out quite far.'

'Not you?'

'No.' Marisa sighed. 'It was another source of argument. Princesses don't swim. My parents didn't want me to be photographed in a swimming costume, but even if I was willing to accept that, which I wasn't, I couldn't see why I couldn't learn how to swim on a private beach with Rohan. My mother said that she had never learnt to swim and seemed to think that clinched the argument.'

He could hear remembered frustration in her voice, 'That must have been annoying, watching Rohan swim out to sea with your dad.'

'It was. Once I sneaked out here and decided to give it a go. So off I went. Thankfully Amina followed me and she plunged in to rescue me, even though she couldn't swim either. She got us back to shore; she was furious but she didn't tell my parents, though she made me promise I'd never do it again. So since then, all I've done is paddle.'

'Didn't you learn when you were abroad?'

'Nope. I knew if I did get snapped in a swimsuit my parents would take it as a further sign that I was rebelling.' She shook her head. 'That sounds daft but it's how I felt. I spent a lot of my time abroad second-guessing myself.'

Kieran understood that, knew that she must have had her parents' voices in her head, questioning every move. 'What did you do? I know you said you tried to forge a different life but what did that entail?'

Marisa gave a laugh that held a tinge of bitterness. 'The key word there is "tried". I tried lots of different jobs, but nothing stuck. I worked as an aide to an MP—I did love that. She was an amazing woman. She was a true politician, someone who cared about her constituents and cared about her country as well. Then, more recently, I taught dance. I ran Indian dancing classes for adults and children—that was fun.' She shrugged. 'But in the end, I suppose I spent ten years drifting. Looking back, it seems like a waste. Maybe I should have come back to Sarala, made a stand.'

Kieran thought for a minute. 'I disagree. I think you would have learnt a lot from those years. Working for a politician will have given you key political skills that will help you navigate the system here. Running dance classes will have given you business skills, and, more importantly, both jobs will have taught you people skills. How to be a modern ruler, truly in touch with your people.'

'Do you mean that?'

'Yes. When I showed you the pictures of the house yesterday you made me see that, without realising it, I'd spent the past eighteen months learning new skills. That's what you did too.'

He rose to his feet. 'How about learning a new skill right now? How about I teach you to swim? And one day we will teach our children to swim whether they are girls or boys.'

Her eyes widened. 'Children?'

The word had come without thought and now he nodded. 'Yes. Children. I'd like more than one child, if you would? I always wished for a sibling and I'd love a large family. But only if that's what you want.'

'That is what I want. Siblings who grow up together without resentment. If there are rules and traditions, then I want to make sure we explain them rather than enforce them.'

'Yes, and if we can bend them or compromise then I always will. And I promise I will always treat them equally.'

'So will I. And I love the idea of teaching them to swim. I can see it now. All of us swimming out a little way...

'The children in armbands and with floats, and we'll be there keeping them safe.'

He could picture it too, another scene taking shape of a possible future. He held out a hand. 'Come on, let's go in a little way.'

She put her hand in his and somehow the gesture felt symbolic as they walked forward together, moving deeper and deeper into the water until she came to a stop and turned to look at him in question.

'I thought you could float on your back. I'll hold on so you'll be supported to begin with.'

Marisa nodded and gently he tipped her over so she was lying on her back in the water, looking up at the sky. 'It's the baby's first lesson as well,' she said with a smile and the words caused a sudden surge of pride, a knowledge that this moment was, oh, so precious, and the sense of connection he felt when she placed her hand on her tummy twisted his chest with warmth.

And when, after a few minutes, he let Marisa go, watched her float by herself, saw her face break into a massive smile that lit her features, something perilously akin to pure happiness washed over him.

'That was awesome,' she said, once they had returned to the beach and were sitting on towels on the sand with the warmth of the sun on their backs. He could already feel the T-shirt drying on his back. 'Thank you. This is turning into a perfect day.'

And it continued the same way as they lazed in the sun, discussed their favourite films, talked about anything and nothing, ate and drank and walked along the golden sands until evening drew in and, hand in hand, they headed back to the house. As they did so Kieran glanced backwards, one quick look at the now darkening sea, shining orange in the rays of the setting sun, and he knew he'd hold this day in his memory banks.

CHAPTER TWELVE

As THEY RE-ENTERED the house Marisa was aware of a different type of tiredness from the day before. This was more of a contented drowsiness, the sort of tiredness where all that she wanted to do was sit in front of a movie and snuggle up to Kieran and...

Whoa.

Where was she going with this? Clearly she *was* tired *and* delusional. Because yes, today they had discussed a real future, but it had been a future centred around children, around a family. And that was enough.

'I'm shattered,' she said. She spotted a note on the hallway table and picked it up. 'Amina says she has got the master bedroom ready.' She glanced at him and suddenly the drowsy contentment started to fade, replaced by a string of questions. How were they going to work out sleeping arrangements? Did she really want to keep the attraction sidelined? If so, how long for? How would this work?

They climbed the stairs in silence and she was preternaturally aware of the beat of her heart as she pushed open the door to the master bedroom and gave a small gasp.

The room had been decked out to welcome a honeymooning couple. A profusion of flowers in vases burst with colour on the table and the windowsills, and flowers garlanded the four-poster bed. The duvet had flower petals strewn on it and a bottle of sparkling locally made lemonade was in a cooler along with a heart-shaped box of chocolates.

'Oh.'

There was a letter on the table and she opened it

Dear Marisa and Kieran,
I wish you all happiness in your marriage.
Blessings and love,
Amina

Marisa blinked back a sudden unexpected threat of tears and handed Kieran the letter to read.

'I have no idea why this is making me cry.'

Unless it was because, for a ridiculous moment, she wanted it to be real. A real marriage that warranted rose petals and flowers and satin sheets and bubbles and chocolates. Not a marriage that solely centred around family. She wanted a real marriage that had been undertaken for them. For Kieran and Marisa. Husband and wife. But it wasn't.

Instead, this was something she would take pictures of and use to bolster an illusion of love.

And that was how it was; any other hopes were naïve and foolish, an echo of the ones she'd harboured all those years ago for Lakshan when she'd allowed herself to get lost in a morass of romantic dreams, lost in her feelings for a man. She would not let that happen again, had to differentiate between fantasy and reality, keep her feelings in check.

'Sorry. Pregnancy hormones,' she said, seeing him study her expression, unable to bear the mortification of him working out her thoughts. 'Amina has just put so much effort into this. And we won't even sleep in the bed.'

Kieran came over to her, hesitated and then took one of her hands in his. 'Actually, I think we should both sleep in here tonight. Amina is a perceptive woman. If I or we sleep somewhere different she will know, however careful we are. So, you sleep in the bed and I'll sleep in a chair in here.'

Irrational hurt struck that he didn't want to sleep in the bed with her, even as she knew he was respecting her request from the previous day, honouring the agreement they had made. Knew he was right to be thinking practically of further ways of bolstering the illusion. Well, so could she.

'I agree we should sleep in here but I think you should sleep in the bed as well. You can't keep sleeping in a chair and realistically we are going to end up sleeping in palace accommodation a lot. There will always be signs. So, we'll need to figure out how to share a bed.'

They both stared at the bed.

'It's pretty big,' Kieran said.

'Exactly. And we can always do what Amina told Rohan and me to do to stop us from fighting when we were kids. Have a pretend barrier between us, that we aren't allowed to broach.'

Did it work?'

She did a so-so gesture with her hand. 'It depended what we were fighting about.'

'It's worth a try.'

Marisa nodded. 'I guess then I'll get ready for bed.'

'Sure. I'll go downstairs, leave you to it.'

Marisa smiled thankfully, aware that, ridiculous though it sounded given the nights they had shared together, the intimacies and the passion, the idea of doing mundane things like moisturising or brushing her hair in front of Kieran seemed even more intimate. And yet they were things she would have to get used to. She hurried through her nightly routine, not wanting to be caught out, and tried to decide what to do next. Read a book in bed, or pretend to be asleep?

In the end she settled for the book option, waited until he came up, watched as he closed the door and then sat at the desk, opened his laptop and soon seemed immersed in something. Marisa tried to focus on the book, but couldn't, so she slid under the blanket and tried to will her body to relax. Reminding herself that just a few hours ago they had been completely natural together, hand in hand. Recalling how he'd held her in the water.

Big mistake. Because now she could almost feel his hands on her back, his touch through the thin wet cotton, and that triggered other memories of those hands on her body, on her bare skin. She shifted, tried to mask the movement, swallowed a sigh. This was ridiculous, but by an effort of will she kept her eyes closed, kept her breathing slow and even, knew Kieran wouldn't get in until he believed her to be asleep.

She maintained the rhythm when he did finally climb in. He was so close; all she would have to do was reach out a hand, and how she wanted to, and in the end she did. Surely that was all right after the day they'd shared, the perfect day on the beach? But as her hand found his she had a sudden fear of rejection, sure he would repudiate her crossing of the barrier. But he didn't, he took her hand in his and finally she felt sleep coming. Knew there was a small goofy smile on her face, hoped there was one on his.

She wasn't sure what woke her up, but as she opened her eyes she glanced towards the window and recognised the early dawn of a Saralan sunrise. She realised that in her sleep she'd shifted closer to Kieran, felt the warm bulk of his body next to hers. So much for the barrier.

He moved, the movement jerky, and his breathing seemed broken, uneven as he shifted. He gave a small groan, and then a shout and then a sudden keening cry. 'No. Aisla. No. Oh, God. I'm sorry, so sorry. I won't. I know. The baby. I'm sorry. Aisla...'

So much more anguish even than two nights before, as if his pain and grief had escalated, and all Marisa wanted to do was soothe him, wake him up gently, tell him it would all be all right, that her love would make everything better.

She froze, her hand still raised to gently wake him.

Her love?

Love.

No, no, no. She did not love Kieran, could not have fallen for an illusion again. Not this time. She could not be that foolish; to fall in love with a man who was grieving, a widower who was still in love with the wife he'd lost. She could see the sweat on his brow, the clench of his hands in the sheets, knew this to be a demonstration of raw grief.

As quietly as she could she slipped from the bed, grabbed her clothes and tiptoed out, barely aware of the tears seeping down her cheeks as she understood what she had to do.

Kieran opened his eyes, looked at the window and saw early morning sunlight stream through, glanced at his watch, saw it was still early, turned his head, reached out, saw the bed was cold, that once again Marisa had got up early. He frowned, blinked, aware his head felt a bit fuzzy, and he shook his head to clear it, suddenly irrationally worried as to where Marisa was.

Swiftly he swung himself out of bed, tugged

on jeans and a T-shirt and left the room. A quick look round showed no sign of Marisa and after a moment's thought Kieran headed out of the house. Maybe she'd gone to the beach? His hunch was rewarded as he approached the golden stretch of sand, and saw her sitting on the sand looking out at the waves. The same spot where they'd sat the day before.

He strode towards her, barely even registering the coolness of the sand under his toes, the heat of the sun and the light blue of the cloudless sky.

She turned as he approached.

'Are you OK?' he asked, looking at her face and seeing that her brown eyes were shadowed.

'I couldn't sleep so I came here to think.'

'Good thoughts?'

'Right thoughts.' She waited as he sat down beside her, stretched his legs out and looked out at the waves, at the horizon. 'For the first time since I discovered I'm pregnant, I stopped thinking about myself. These past weeks I have been so caught up in the panic, in the need to do the right thing for Sarala and the baby and myself, that I haven't been thinking straight. Or perhaps more importantly I haven't been thinking of you. And I'm sorry. Truly sorry.'

A sense of foreboding touched him. 'That's

not true. You were thinking of me. You told
me about the baby.'

'Not really. I sent Amit to get you, without
even telling you why. If I had been thinking
about you, I'd have got on the plane and come
and told you myself.'

'Which would have been foolish, given the
situation here, given you had no idea what sort
of man I am.'

Marisa gave a small smile. 'Thank you.
That is kind. You have proven over and over
again that you are a kind man, but that's not
the point. I haven't thought about what this
marriage, this situation, is doing to you. I understand that you love our baby and want to be
the best possible father but I effectively gave
you little choice but to handle this pregnancy
my way. You have had to pay for the consequences of my decisions.'

'Our decisions,' he said. 'That night. The
night that created our baby—we were both
there, we both chose.'

'Yes, but I knew what was at stake. The risks
I took were higher because the stakes were
higher for me. You're paying for that. I have
forced you into a marriage you don't want.'
She raised a hand. 'I know you want to be
there for our child, but you would have been

happy to work out joint custody. That is what
you wanted. Instead, you married me.'

Different emotions were beginning to swirl
round inside him, emotions he was having difficulty identifying. Marisa was correct. That
was what he had wanted. And now? Now it
didn't matter what he *wanted*. He'd done the
right thing for Marisa and the baby. That was
what mattered.

'I didn't have to agree to this marriage.'

'No. But I didn't give you a lot of choice.
And you don't want to be married. You lost
your wife, a wife you still love and grieve
and miss.' Her voice broke slightly and guilt
slammed into him, guilt that he'd let her believe a version of the truth.

'I…'

'It's OK, Kieran. You don't have to try to
find a nice way to explain it. I know.' She took
a deep breath. 'You've been having nightmares.'

Kieran stilled. He should have known, recognised the signs. The heavy head, the clammy
feeling.

'You called out to Aisla, said how sorry you
were, you even mentioned the baby.'

Her words were like a sucker punch. The
baby, not her baby, not their baby growing inside her, but a different baby, the one he felt

he was replacing, even though he knew with his head that he wasn't, it didn't work like that. And now words wouldn't come.

'I get it. You lost your wife, the woman you loved, the woman you truly wanted to spend the rest of your life with. Being with me…it must feel like a betrayal, of her. Of the love you had for her.'

'It's not like that.' The words ripped from him were carried hoarse and rasping on the sea breeze.

'It is like that and I want to make amends. I should never have made you do this and now I release you. I know I can't release you immediately, but I promise I'll work out a way. Somehow. And while I do, we'll maintain an illusion but we'll live separate lives. I hope that in some way assuages your guilt, makes it easier to live with this marriage.'

Kieran knew he had to stop this now. That he couldn't let her believe what she believed. He could see the brightness of unshed tears in her brown eyes and his chest twisted with the knowledge that he'd hurt her. Created an illusion to protect Aisla's memory. At the time the illusion had seemed right, acceptable. But now it seemed so very wrong.

'Wait. Marisa. Please listen to me. I need to tell you the truth. About my marriage and about Aisla's death. There are things you need to know.'

'You don't need to tell me anything.' Her voice was soft. 'Truly. I just wanted you to know that I am sorry and that I understand.'

'There is no need for you to be sorry. As for understanding, you don't and that's my fault.'

She remained silent, her back ramrod straight, and she looked away from him, out to sea, at the blue waves lapping the shore, and now the sun beat down a little bit hotter, a tattoo of heat, as he tried to work out what to say and where to start.

'I met Aisla when we were both in our last year of university. At a party. I wasn't really much of a partygoer. Even then Mark, Lucy and I were a tight-knit unit. We were too immersed in planning our company, figuring out what to do and how to do it. But Lucy decided we needed to network more; said the more contacts we had, the better it would be in the future. So, we went and that's where I met Aisla. She was…' He paused and Marisa leaned forward slightly.

'It's OK. Tell me what she was like. That's a good way of remembering her. When my grandfather died one of the best things we did was to remember him, talk about what he was like. Shared memories show our respect and love for those who have passed and it's a way of keeping their memories alive.'

'She was a person with convictions. Some people thought she was opinionated or even abrasive, but I saw a person who really believed in things.' He'd thought she was like him, ambitious, focused, passionate about following a dream. For a moment he could see the woman he'd seen then, red hair, green eyes, petite. 'She was studying interior design, though she said her heart wasn't really in it. We became a couple and a few weeks later we got engaged.' He met Marisa's eyes. 'My parents, my friends, all had reservations. Thought we should wait a while.'

He recalled his mum's voice, gentle, laced with an edge of worry, but trying to sound reasonable and non-antagonistic. 'Don't you think it's a little quick, sweetheart? You barely know each other and...' She'd broken off and Kieran had waited.

'And what?' he'd asked, his tone full of belligerence.

'And it's a massive step, a huge commitment. Wouldn't it be better to wait, make sure and—?'

'You don't like her.' His voice had been flat.

'I do like her,' his mum had protested. 'But I don't really know her and, anyway, me liking her doesn't make her the right person for you or you the right person for her.'

'So you don't think we're right for each other?'

'I didn't say that. I just don't think you can know.'

Kieran blinked away the memory, refocused on Marisa.

'But, of course, we didn't listen and the wedding went ahead. That's why their relationship with Aisla was complicated: she always believed they didn't like her no matter what they did.' And his parents had tried, accepted the marriage and done everything they could to welcome Aisla into the family. But Aisla hadn't wanted that, had flatly refused to be any more than barely civil, the politeness bordering on rudeness, a trace of exasperation in her voice, a roll of the eyes making everything awkward.

And, of course, he'd taken her side. It was only later that it had occurred to him that there shouldn't have needed to be sides. His parents had never once shown Aisla anything but kindness, warmth and courtesy. But after the wedding Aisla had somehow always made excuses not to see his parents, had been upset when he'd gone to see them and so, slowly, he and his parents had grown apart.

'But...' He paused, looked at Marisa's face;

there was no judgement, no prurient curiosity, simply a focus on his words. 'As time went on, it became clear that Aisla and I were very different, and while that doesn't have to be an issue in a relationship, in ours it was. She started to resent the time I spent at work, wanted me to give up on the idea of starting a business with Mark and Lucy, said she thought it was a young person's ridiculous pipe dream. An excuse to spend time with my friends. But it was more than that...we didn't seem to agree on anything and it all got worse. Silly arguments, and deeper ones...' He stopped.

'I did try, truly I did, but I couldn't seem to get it right.' If he'd brought home flowers, they'd been the wrong ones. If he'd done something on Valentine's Day he'd been bowing to the commercial gods. If he hadn't it had meant he was thoughtless. 'Perhaps I should have given up Mix It Up, it did take a lot of my time, but—'

'But that was your dream,' Marisa said. 'That ambition, that drive, that dream would have made you the person you were, the person she married.'

He shook his head. 'I don't think either of us knew the person we married. We mistook attraction and sparks for love and it wasn't.' It was the first time he'd said the words out loud.

'We made a mistake; I wanted to try counsel-
ling but Aisla didn't believe in it. I suggested
a break, a trial separation, but she didn't want
that either.' His voice caught. 'I even caught
myself thinking maybe I should move out for
a while, force a break. Then...'

He hesitated, pushed his fingers hard into
the sand. 'Then one day she came and told me
she was pregnant; it wasn't planned, but she
thought it would solve all our problems. That a
baby would mean I had to stay at home more,
would bind us together. She said that if I didn't
give this a go, she'd try to get sole custody, but
what she really wanted was for us to be happy.'
The stick-and-carrot approach.

'I agreed, because I hoped she was right,
hoped that the baby would solve everything,
that also, once I made it, she'd see I was right,
that she'd love the money, the lifestyle, everything. But nothing worked out like that. The
accident happened and Aisla and our unborn
baby both died. I let down my wife and my
baby. That's what my nightmares are about.'

There was a silence and to his relief Marisa
made no move to reach out.

When she spoke, her voice was low and he
could hear the pain in it. 'I am so very, very
sorry for your loss. To lose an unborn child
like that as well as your wife, whatever state

your marriage was in, is an unspeakable tragedy and I am truly so very sorry.' She took a
deep breath and he sensed her gaze on him as
he continued to look out to sea. 'I understand
how searing the grief must have been, must
still be... But I don't understand why you think
you let them down. You stuck to a marriage
you had doubts about, for the sake of the baby.
You were trying to make it work, doing your
best for them.'

'Because I should have been driving. I knew
Aisla was tired, and I should have insisted, but
when I tried, she started on about women being
better drivers and it being proven and so I let it
go. But if I'd insisted, maybe she would have
agreed, and if I'd been driving, she and the
baby would have survived, or maybe, maybe
I'd have seen the lorry coming.'

'Or you may all have died, or more people
may have died or... There are so many might-
have-beens, so many permutations that you
simply can't compute. I know you must sometimes wish it had been you, but it wasn't. That
is not your fault. You can't take on that burden
of responsibility.'

Now he did turn to look at her. 'But I can
take responsibility for being a bad husband. I
made the last years of Aisla's life miserable.
All she wanted of me was that I should spend

more time with her, be a better husband, and I wasn't willing to do that. If I wasn't willing to change then I should have had the courage of my convictions and made a clean break of it, accepted I made, *we* made, a mistake. The bottom line is she wasn't happy in our marriage, and now she won't have the chance to be happy at all.'

'If she wasn't happy she could have left. She chose not to. She chose a different way and maybe her way would have worked, maybe you'd have worked it out. Or perhaps you wouldn't. But I do know something.' Now she did reach out and covered his hand with hers. 'Yesterday you showed me perspective. You need to do the same for yourself. I don't believe your whole time with Aisla was miserable—or that she was miserable all the time. There must have been something she wanted to salvage and I bet especially those last months she was happy, looking forward to being a mum, being a family with you. And your baby... I am so sorry, so sorry for your loss and how that loss must be making you feel now, about our baby. But I also know that you would have been a wonderful father to that baby, just as you will be to our baby.'

A warmth touched him at the simple sincerity of her words and he let his hand rest in hers.

'Next time I am in the temple I will say a prayer for the soul of your lost baby and place an offering of flowers for it,' she said softly.

'Thank you.'

They sat for a while and then she took a deep breath.

'Thank you for sharing that with me, and now we need to talk about the future.'

He looked across at her, wanting to close down a conversation he knew he didn't want. He wanted the future to continue as planned, for their marriage, their partnership to keep on going. Perhaps made stronger by what they had just shared. But perhaps that wasn't what Marisa wanted and if she didn't want that then he would give her whatever she wanted to make her happy. This time he would do the right thing at whatever cost to himself.

CHAPTER THIRTEEN

MARISA TRIED TO analyse the swirling thoughts in her brain—her deep sorrow for Kieran and what he had gone through, the urge to offer comfort, to help, to be by his side and try to make everything better. Her heart twisted. Losing a baby…the very idea chilled her soul. But more than that, she knew that what she wanted to give him was the one thing she mustn't. She wanted to offer love. Because as she'd sat on this beach, as she'd stared out to sea knowing that in the bedroom they shared he was grieving his lost wife, she'd accepted the foolish thing she'd done. She'd fallen in love with him. A man who didn't love her back and must never be burdened with the knowledge that she loved him. A man who she had to free.

A decision fortified and consolidated by everything he'd just shared.

Aisla had manipulated him into remaining in a marriage that had been a mistake, used their baby as a bargaining chip. When she'd heard that, Marisa had been horrified until she'd realised it was exactly what she'd done herself.

Aisla at least had had a reason: a marriage to save, a love that had once existed.

Marisa had had nothing but her own selfish needs. Needs she'd allowed to trump the voice of doubt that had told her he had agreed too easily, had pointed out all he was giving up: his country, his life, his family.

Well, no more.

'I stand by what I said earlier. Perhaps you don't feel as though you are betraying Aisla's love, but you are trying to do the right thing for the wrong reasons.' She saw his frown and raised her hand. 'I'm not explaining this very well. You deserve happiness, Kieran. True happiness. What you are doing with me is creating an illusion of happiness, and that isn't right. And because you are a good person, and perhaps because you feel that you let Aisla down, you are trying to make up for that with me. Everything you have done these past days, all the kind, thoughtful things…' perhaps humiliating enough, perhaps even the time in bed '…were to make me happy.'

'Is that so bad? I do want you to be happy.'

'But what about you? You need a chance at

happiness. You deserve a chance at happiness.'
He'd said that Aisla had had that chance taken
from her. Marisa understood now that Kieran
believed that meant he didn't deserve a chance
either. That was why he'd fallen in with her
idea so readily; he believed his own happiness
to be unimportant, unwanted, undeserved.

'Once you married for love. You deserve
the chance to do that again. If that's what you
want. You deserve the chance to complete your
house in Scotland, to live your life how you
want to live it. Not here with me because you
feel you should. You will be a wonderful dad,
whether you are married to me or not.'

She inhaled deeply. 'As for me, I need to
have my happy ending.' She willed herself to
hold his gaze. Even as she knew what she was
saying was a lie, a barefaced lie. But somehow, she'd make it truth. 'The one where I rule,
where I sit on the throne and rule alone.' Once
the very apex of her desires and now it felt
empty. 'As I said, it will take time. But I've
decided what I'm going to do. I'm going to
postpone the coronation; the people and my
parents have asked for time. I am going to ask
for a year to prove myself, a year to show I am
a true ruler.'

And she would do her best, still wanted
to show her people what she was capable of,

wanted to help her country. But now she wanted more, wanted it all. Well, she couldn't have that and wasn't going to manipulate or force Kieran into staying in yet another mistaken marriage. 'I think you should go back to Scotland, back to your life for a while. I can explain that an emergency has come up. We can cast another illusory spell.'

She stopped now, waited for him to say something. Aware that a tiny bit of her was hoping that he'd tell her that he wouldn't go, that he wanted this marriage, wanted it because he loved her. That he chose her, not for the baby, not for Sarala, not because it was the right thing to do, but because he loved her. But, of course, he wouldn't. She knew that.

He ran a hand over his face, his expression almost stunned, and for once she could see indecision etched on his features as he studied her expression and she forced herself to keep her face calm, regal. As if now her decision was made, she was ready to move on.

'So, this is what you truly want? Now you have secured our child's birthright, you want to rule alone? To have a marriage that is in name only until we can work out a way to dissolve it?'

There was both hurt and confusion on his face and it occurred to her that perhaps he thought that was what she had planned all along, that the days they had spent together had been a true illusion, the type woven by Lakshan. Or perhaps he believed he'd done something wrong, that he had precipitated her decision. And she wanted to cry out, refute her own words, ask him to stay. But that would be wrong; better he believed anything than the truth. That she was freeing him because it was the only way she could show her love, her realisation that he had his own life to lead.

'Yes, that is what I want,' she said steadily. Perhaps the words weren't real today but, somehow, she'd make them true. 'We made a mistake; we should accept that now.'

'But you agree that I will co-parent, that I will be our child's father, properly? Joint custody. Equal rights, shared time…'

'I agree. I swear to you I will never keep our baby from you.'

'Then so be it,' he said, and she looked for some relief in his voice, saw nothing but a bleakness that dimmed the intensity of his blue eyes.

'This is the right thing to do,' she said, trying to keep the bleakness from her own voice, terrified he'd guess the truth, hear the crack of her heart. 'You deserve happiness, Kieran. I will be grateful for ever for what you have done for me and for Sarala, but now you are entitled to your own life. I will free you, I promise.'

Scotland,
two weeks later

Kieran pulled a jumper over his head and looked out at the faint tendrils of sun that sent a wash of pale sunlight over the mountainous Scottish landscape, highlighting the browns and greens and gorse and bracken. The beauty here was different from that of Sarala, but it was beautiful nonetheless and he wished Marisa were here to see it. But she wasn't and she would never be. However often he had told himself that in the past days his brain wouldn't accept it.

Instead, as he walked from room to room, he heard her voice in his head, admiring what he'd done, making him see the progress he'd made as an achievement, giving him words of advice. So now as he looked at the walls, studied the curve of the staircase, he felt a sense of pride and in his mind's eye he could see a completed house, could see Marisa standing at the top of the stairs, Marisa sitting in the kitchen while he cooked, and in her arms was the swaddled form of a baby.

But that was not happening.

Because it wasn't what Marisa wanted. It was not her dream. He'd always known that, hadn't he? Right from the start—it was about Sarala. Her happy ending was to rule alone and he wanted her to have that dream. He accepted her words and the rejection implicit in them; after all, she was doing what he should have done all those years ago, accepting she'd made a mistake in thinking they could make a go of it and cutting loose without wasting further time. Marisa knew what she wanted and he would respect that, would not make her unhappy as he had Aisla.

He would still have the chance to be a proper hands-on father, would still be part of his child's life, and that *was* what he wanted. So why did everything feel so bleak? Why did what should feel like a win-win situation feel so very wrong?

A knock on the front door provided a welcome distraction and he headed to open it, pulled the door open and saw his parents, standing together, their faces wreathed in cautious smiles, the same note of caution he'd heard in his mum's voice when he'd called to ask them to visit.

There was a small hesitation and then his mum made a small noise, a pfft, as she said, 'To hell with it,' stepped forward and wrapped her arms round him in a hug.

For a second, he tensed, as the instinct honed by years of grieving, of rejecting human warmth, kicked in. Then a memory of holding Marisa, *offering* comfort, filled his mind, along with other images from the past week, of holding hands, walking, arms round each other's waists, and so, instead of pulling away, he relaxed into his mum's embrace. He returned the hug and heard her small sigh of surprise, a catch of her breath, and when she finally released him, he saw the suspicion of a tear glint in her blue eyes.

Then his dad stepped forward, shook his hand and then enveloped him in a bear hug before standing back. 'Well, what are we waiting for? Show us round and then your mum's brought enough provisions to feed an army.'

After the tour Kieran saw his dad hadn't been exaggerating and soon they were sitting at his makeshift kitchen table, spread with pasties, pies, cold meats, cheese, and different types of bread, interspersed with pickles, chutneys and salad.

His eyes rested on a jar of lime pickle and he pictured Marisa, dipping a banana chip into it and handing it over, her smiling face, the sparkle in her brown eyes. Then just days later sitting at the beach, her brown eyes shadowed, telling him it was all over.

How had he managed to mess it all up again?

'Kieran?' His mum's voice was quiet. 'Do you want to talk about it? You can trust us.'

He met her gaze, knew she spoke truth. Knew his parents had only ever had his happiness at heart, that he could trust them to listen and give advice that came from their own hearts.

'There isn't much to say,' he said quietly. 'I met Marisa three months ago. For one date. I didn't know she was a princess, didn't know anything about her.' Yet now he knew so much. How she smiled, how she liked her coffee, her love for chillies, the intense concentration she brought to a situation, her passion, her vulner-abilities.

'She fell pregnant and she asked me to marry her so our child could be legitimate, and could succeed to the Saralan throne. I agreed. I thought we could actually make a go of it, that I could make her happy. But I can't. So, we will put a brave face on it for a while. I will be part of my child's life and eventually we'll figure out a way to separate.'

There was a silence, then his mum frowned. 'Is that what you want? It doesn't sound that way to me.'

'It doesn't matter what I want.' He'd ignored what Aisla wanted, failed as a husband once— he wouldn't do that again.

'So, it's what Marisa wants? Are you sure?'

'Ye—' Kieran broke off. Was he sure? Of course he was. Was he? He looked back, recalled the determination on her face, the remote regal expression. Yet she hadn't looked happy, her voice had been firm but underlaid with bleakness. And did her decision make any sense?

'What I mean is, if you both had agreed you thought it could work, something must have changed.' His mother's question now seemed so obvious. She was right. They had agreed, and now memories began to filter through his brain, through the barrier of bleakness, the grim focus of the past fortnight of fatalistic acceptance of her decision.

But now his hand went up to the chain around his neck and he could remember the way she'd given it to him, recalled their conversation about a family, their plans for swimming lessons, for a future together, her hand finding his in sleep, crossing the make-believe barrier.

All that had not been an illusion. So, what had changed? He'd told her about Aisla, about the baby, but she'd already made her decision, before that. What had she said—she'd said she should never have forced him into marriage. He'd been so focused on the part where she'd said she wanted to correct the mistake, rule alone, that he hadn't really thought about *why* she thought it was a mistake.

Absent-mindedly he picked up a slice of bread, put it down, moved some crumbs round and now his brain started to fizz, to pop, to ask questions, analyse...*think*. 'I... Marisa said I deserve happiness.' He was an idiot. She believed he had married her only for the baby. He had done that, but that had been then and, dammit, this was now.

'Are you happy?' his mum asked.

'No.'

'Why not?' This time it was his dad who asked the question, his voice gentle, and he was answering instinctively now.

'Because I miss her, because I love her.'

He stared at his parents, the realisation so blindingly obvious and yet so new, so stunning, that all he could do was sit there and absorb it as the truth it was. He loved Marisa. He waited for the hammer blow of guilt, the need to weed out the feelings, but instead he felt nothing but an immense joy.

Couldn't regret this, couldn't help this, couldn't change this. And he didn't want to.

Sarala

Marisa sat at her desk in her new office, or at least one of the many unused rooms in the palace that she had made into her office. Sat and stared at the computer, tried to concentrate on the report in front of her dealing with imports and exports, aware that all she wanted to do was discuss it with Kieran.

Talk about the best way to promote Saralan goods. Perhaps he would suggest people dressing up as mangos or silkworms… She reached out for a banana chip and there it was again, another memory of Kieran. An image of their wedding meal, an image of what had happened afterwards, and she found tears springing to her eyes as she inadvertently hummed the jazz song they'd danced to.

Enough.

That had been an illusion, a man making up for his past marriage, trying to do good to cancel out a perceived past wrong.

Somehow, she had to pull herself together. Kieran would be back in a week or so. Back so they could continue the illusion. Only now every part of that pretence would bring her pain, the poignancy of might-have-beens and impossible wishes already haunting her waking dreams.

'Risa?'

She opened her eyes, blinked fiercely and attempted a smile as she saw her brother, surprised by the use of her childhood nickname he hadn't used for years.

'Hey, little bro.'

'What's wrong?' he asked. 'Is it Kieran? If it is I'll—'

'It's not Kieran.' She swiped her eye and sat up straight. No way was she letting Kieran take the blame for this.

'Then why has he gone to Scotland? And don't give me any half-baked story about needing to get things tied up. Has he ratted out? Is being married to a princess a bit harder work than he thought? Is—?'

'Stop. Please, Ro-Ro, just stop. It's not Kieran's fault. I made him go.'

Rohan raised his eyebrows. 'Kieran didn't strike me as a man you could make do anything.'

'OK, then. It was my idea and he agreed. Because he thought that's what I wanted.' She saw Rohan's look. 'I mean, it *is* what I wanted.'

'Why? Not that I believe you, but tell me anyway.'

'I did want him to go,' she said.

'Come on, Risa, tell me. Please. I know we don't talk about things in this family but maybe it's time we started. Maybe I can help—like you helped me, when you told me to fix things with Elora.'

'That wasn't exactly a talk,' she said with a small smile. 'It was more me being bossy and stating the obvious.' Telling her brother to fix things with the woman he clearly loved.

'Well, it helped and I'd like to return the favour. So, tell me. The truth.'

Maybe Rohan was right; it was time to start behaving like a real family. Kieran had told her he could talk to his parents about anything without judgement. And right now, she didn't feel she had anything to lose. 'Kieran and I had one night together; it was never meant to be more than that. Then I found out that I am pregnant.' She heard his small intake of breath but he said nothing, waited for her to continue. 'I persuaded him, *manipulated* him into marrying me. He did it for the baby. It was wrong of me and I am trying to make amends, work out how to free him.'

'But in the meantime, you've fallen in love with him?'

'Yes.' There seemed little point in a denial she knew her brother would see through.

'Then tell him.'

'I can't. It's not fair to him... He never meant to hurt me. He would try to make this work and I can't let him do that.' Be stuck in another loveless marriage, where he couldn't follow his dreams.

'I still think you should tell him.'

'I agree with Rohan.' Marisa gave a small

start of surprise as she heard her mother's voice from the doorway. 'I'm sorry. I did not mean to listen.'

How much had her mother heard? She studied the Queen's face, saw no trace of anger and she could only assume she really had only heard the last few words, though she also knew her mother was perfectly capable at listening at the door if it was for the good of Sarala. In fact, she was surprised she'd even bothered to apologise.

'But now that I did hear I do agree with your brother. Of course you need to make this work.'

'For the sake of Sarala? Because if we admit we made a mistake then there will be another scandal? I understand all that and so does Kieran. We will put on a show, make it look as though things are OK for a while, but I have promised I will work towards giving him his freedom back.'

'Why?'

Marisa looked at her mother. 'Because it's not fair to ask Kieran to sacrifice his life for the sake of Sarala. We made a mistake—he shouldn't have to pay for it.'

'I am not only speaking for Sarala's sake. But for yours. You love him.'

'Exactly. So, I want him to be happy.'

'He looked pretty happy to me,' her mother said tartly. 'With you.'

'That was for the camera, an illusion.'

'Then make it real.'

'I can't. I can't make him love me.' Couldn't drag him kicking and screaming into love.

'But you can try. You said that you are going to stay together for the sake of Sarala for a while. Then make that time count, don't just give up.'

Marisa frowned as she looked at her mother. She couldn't work out if her mother was telling her this for Sarala or for her daughter. And suddenly realised perhaps it didn't matter, perhaps her mother didn't know herself. But she was trying.

'Thank you, Amma. I will think about what you've said. What you've both said.'

Her mother nodded. 'Don't throw something positive away unless you are absolutely sure it is the right thing to do.' She hesitated. 'Once I nearly refused to marry your father.'

Both Rohan and Marisa stared at their mother, who gave a sudden smile. 'I was young once too, I had ideas and beliefs, and I knew your father was actually in love with my sister. But she was betrothed to someone else, an excellent marriage for my family, an alliance that could not be changed. He accepted this and our marriage was arranged. But I did not want it.'

'Of course you didn't,' Marisa said. 'Why did you do it?'

'Because in the end I played the long game.' Marisa blinked in surprise—the same words that Kieran had used. 'I knew your father was a good man. I knew too that he and my sister would not have been happy. She was beautiful but she was not interested in politics or duty—they wouldn't have worked. I saw a man who I could love and I hoped that one day he would love me. Perhaps it isn't romantic, perhaps it's not a fairy tale, but it worked. Your father and I are happy. Together. And we do love each other.'

Marisa walked around her desk and over to her mother, and for the first time in as long as she could remember she hugged her.

'Thank you, Amma.'

And then Rohan was there too, and for a brief moment they all hugged before stepping back. Marisa could see her own embarrassment reflected in Rohan's slightly sheepish smile, but, despite the unfamiliarity of the gesture, Marisa felt a sense of warmth and she'd swear the Queen had a glint of a tear in her brown eyes.

'Well.' Queen Kaamini cleared her throat.

'I will leave you to it. I hope you make a good decision.'

Once she had gone Marisa looked at Rohan, whose grin had broadened. 'Well,' he repeated. 'I hope you make a good decision too. Give love a chance, Marisa. I did and I know I'll never regret it.'

With that he was gone and Marisa sat down at her desk, her thoughts whirling as she tried to decide what to do. The answer suddenly obvious.

Pulling out her phone, she messaged Kieran.

I would like to talk if that is OK with you? Is there any chance you could come back to Sarala a few days earlier, or perhaps I could fly to Scotland if that is more convenient for you?

The words felt ridiculously formal but she hit Send anyway, because she knew she'd change her mind if she didn't act now.

She grabbed her phone when it pinged.

I can be there in half an hour. Just landed on Sarala.

Marisa stared down at the message and her tummy twisted with both anticipation and nerves and a sudden moment of sheer happiness.

* * *

Kieran climbed out of the car. 'Thank you, Jai.'

'You're welcome.' The security officer inclined her head. 'And, Kieran? Good luck.'

He smiled his thanks, knew he'd need every bit of luck going, knew what was at stake here, and for a second his step faltered, before he shook his head at his own cowardice. He wouldn't let fear of rejection, fear that he'd mess this up, hold him back. He strode towards the entrance, stopped as a side gate to the gardens opened.

He turned and saw Marisa and he came to a halt. Stood and absorbed the sight of her.

Her hair was loose, cascading in waves of curls to her shoulders, the glossy blackness highlighted by the rays of the bright Saralan sunlight. She wore a long red embroidered tunic over dark leggings.

'Kieran,' she said and he forced himself to move, his senses heightened so that the blue of the sky seemed so light, so bright.

'Marisa. It's good to see you.' The world's biggest understatement. It was better than good; it felt right, made him feel complete. Stop. It didn't matter how he felt; it mattered how Marisa felt. Because no matter what happened here today, he had vowed to himself that he would abide by her wishes.

'You too. I wasn't expecting you today.'

'No.' He left it at that, stood so close to her now that he could smell her shampoo, the vanilla overtones mingled with the scent from the gardens, the proliferation of blooms that shimmered in the sunlit air, bright reds and whites, pinks and blues.

'I've found a place to talk,' she said, and led the way along the path strewn with woodchip, shaded by the dappled green leaves of the banyan trees that flanked it until they came to a small terraced area nestled in a glade, where a table and chairs were laid out. The area was enclosed by a balcony, looking down over another levelled garden, that showed rows and square beds of herbs, as well as plants that sprouted bright red and green chillies. The table held a teapot as well as a selection of snacks and she gave a small rueful smile. 'The chef heard of your arrival and insisted on providing a welcome home offering.'

Home. The word welcome in itself—the knowledge showed an acceptance that he wouldn't have presumed to hope for. But he had no idea if Marisa was simply quoting the chef or stating her own belief.

Perhaps she wasn't sure herself because she flushed slightly, hurried into speech. 'How is Scotland? Have you made progress on the house?'

'A little. I've started to make a table, for the kitchen.' Large enough for a family, he wanted to say. 'I did some other things while I was back.'

'Such as?'

'I did a lot of thinking and that's why I am here. Today. Now. There are things I want to say.'

She nodded. 'There are things I want to say too. But you go first,' she said quickly.

'I want to apologise.' This was the easy bit, the bit that needed to be said first. 'I should never have lied about my marriage to Aisla, should never have let you believe it was an idyllic union.'

'You didn't lie. I assumed.'

'Advertising semantics,' he said with a small smile, reminding her of her words to him weeks before. 'I didn't lie, but I allowed you to believe an illusion I created because I thought that honoured Aisla's memory. I believed I failed her as a husband so the least I could do was create a mythical, perfect marriage. But you made me see that what I did was wrong, that I'd betrayed Aisla more because I wasn't remembering the person she truly was, wasn't remembering her actual life. Our marriage was far from perfect, but it existed, it was ours, hers and mine. And Aisla was the person she was and that is how she should be remembered and grieved.

'And you deserved to know the truth and not to believe that I was still in love with Aisla. I wasn't. What Aisla and I had—we believed it was love, but it wasn't. That's why we couldn't make it work. We didn't have a foundation to build on, didn't have all the elements you need to balance a marriage.' His hands went up to touch the necklace around his neck.

Marisa's eyes followed the gesture. 'But maybe you would have managed to start again, rebuild on a new foundation as a family?'

'Maybe we would,' he said. 'And I will always grieve that Aisla died so young and I will always grieve for the baby who never had a chance at life. I think recently, those nightmares, the guilt I felt, was to do with that. With the idea that I was being given another chance with another baby. That I was moving on. But what I've realised, these past days, is that it is OK to move on. That is part of life.

'When I started on that house in Scotland I did it because I needed something to do, physical labour to exhaust me. When I started, I didn't care about the house itself. I thought that I never cared. But when I showed you the pictures, the before and after, everything you said made me realise I did care. I learnt new skills, to build, to labour, to create things, to do carpentry, to landscape…and with that house I was building something new. And when I went back I knew I wanted to keep building, but now I wanted to build a home.'

He took a deep breath, saw a shadow flit across her eyes, knew she thought he meant a home for himself, knew he had to speak now.

He opened his mouth to tell her the truth, that he wanted it to be a place for her, for the baby, a family retreat, but before he could speak, she leant forward.

'I am pleased you are moving on, truly I am, and you know I want you to be happy. I have been thinking of ways for you to spend more time at home…away from Sarala and…'

Kieran felt his heart plummet, all his earlier optimism, determination to speak, ebbing away. If Marisa wanted him away as much as possible, if her heart was set on ruling alone, being alone, then perhaps he should keep his feelings to himself.

But they had stood on the *mandap*, touched the seven stones, made vows. They meant something.

'That's not what I want,' he said, and the words reverberated on the heat-laden air. 'I meant that the home I am building... I want it to be a place for us, a family place for you and me and the baby, the child... The children. A place for us to go sometimes, when we want a change of scene, a place where we can be a more normal family, a way we can show our children a different way of life, a different type of beauty.'

He heard the catch of her breath as her eyes widened. 'Family place? I... I don't understand.'

'I want us to be a family. A real family. I want this to be a real marriage. Based on love.'

She half rose to her feet. 'Don't...'

He was messing this up; now he'd distressed her and the knowledge tore his heart. 'I'm sorry... I didn't mean to upset you. I won't say any more.'

Marisa stared at Kieran, saw the concern in his blue eyes and forced herself to sit down again; she wouldn't, couldn't run away from this. Had promised herself she would be honest with him.

She raised a hand. 'Of course, I want to hear your thoughts. I know how much you love our baby and how much you want us to be a family. But you don't have to make a home for us; you need to make a home for yourself. That house in Scotland—it's yours, and of course you can take our child there to stay, but you don't have to try to make us into a loving family. You don't have to take responsibility for my happiness.'

She took a deep breath. 'That's not possible. You weren't responsible for Aisla's happiness—she was. And I don't want you to spend your life worrying about mine. Trying to make our marriage work because you feel you have to, or you owe me anything. Or because of our child. We will both love our baby and we can co-parent.'

'I know that.' His voice was quiet. 'And I know it's not my responsibility to make you happy. I meant… I hoped…' He closed his eyes and then rose to his feet. 'I love you.' He tipped his hands in the air. 'There you go. That's it. I love you.'

Marisa knew she had to say something, but her brain couldn't process the information that was coming in. Kieran loved her—how could that be true? Was it true? Was it real?

'You don't have to say that.'

'I know I don't. I'm saying it because it's true. I love you.'

Could she believe him? Could she let herself? Of course she could, because Kieran didn't lie. She knew that with all her heart and soul because she trusted him. Slowly a sense of joy, of happiness, started to seep through her. 'When I said I wanted to talk I wanted to ask you if you would consider giving our marriage a try, if, while we had to keep the illusion going, we could see if we could make it real, if we could go back to our original plan of seeing if our marriage could work.'

'Why?' His voice was taut now, taut with a hope that she could hear, and it twisted her heart. 'Why were you going to ask me that?'

'Because *I* love *you*.' The words spilled out now in a joyous torrent. 'With all my heart and soul. I love you.'

For a moment they stared at each other, and she could see his smile light up his face, those intense blue eyes bright with happiness and joy, knew her own smile reflected that same happiness and joy. He loved her. She loved him.

'You really love me?' His voice sounded dazed.

'I really do. I knew that awful day on the beach; I knew but I was so sure the right thing to do was to make you leave, give you your freedom, because I wanted you to be happy.'

'And I went because I thought ruling alone is what would make you happy.'

'But these last weeks I have missed you

so much it hurt,' she said, clasping his hands tightly, hardly able to believe that from now on she need never let go. 'All that kept me going was the idea it was the right thing to do. For you. But then Rohan made me see that I hadn't told you the truth, or at least not the full truth. I'd made you believe that I wanted you to go and I didn't. I created another illusion, something that wasn't real. And that wasn't right either, because *I* was making a decision about what was right for *you*. Only you can make that decision. You do deserve happiness, but you also deserve to decide yourself what makes you happy.'

'You make me happy,' he said simply. 'But I have realised that doesn't make you solely responsible for my happiness, just as I am not solely responsible for yours. But our vows, they told us to work together to create a happy union. And that's what I want to do: build our marriage on a foundation of love.'

She nodded. 'And we have all the right elements to keep building on and nurturing our love.'

'We do. Every single one. I know our relationship started with sparks and attraction.' Just as hers had with Lakshan and his with Aisla. 'But we have discovered so much more than that. We work together, we want the other person's happiness, to help them to their dream. We can talk to each other, we can laugh together, confide in each other without fear of judgement. Support each other.' He put his hand in his pocket and pulled out a long oblong box. 'I bought you this.'

She opened the box, aware that her fingers were trembling as she clicked the lid up, looked down at the necklace, a slender gold chain, with seven beaded daisies woven onto it. 'We told a story,' he said. 'Wove an illusion where I gave you a garland of daisies as part of my proposal. I am making that illusion real with this. To me each daisy represents one of the vows we made.'

'Mutual respect, a promise to try and prosper together, to share our wealth and our achievements, raise strong, good children, be faithful, be lifelong partners, work together to create balance, mental, spiritual and physical. Acquire happiness and harmony through mutual love.'

As she said the words she blinked back tears of complete happiness, knew now that they could say and mean every single one of those vows, that their marriage was truly based on mutual love.

'Would you mind putting it on for me?'

'Of course I will.'

He rose and came round to her side of the table and as he clasped it round her neck his fingers brushed the nape of her neck, triggering warmth and desire and a wave of happiness.

She looked up at him. 'So, no more illusions.'

'No more illusions.'

And she knew there would no longer be any need for illusion, because their love was real and true and would last for ever.

EPILOGUE

One year later,
Sarala

MARISA GAZED ROUND the throne room and a wave of happiness washed over her as she looked at her family, everyone sitting around the long table, and now somehow the room was no longer intimidating, the two massive bejewelled thrones still exuded majesty but it was a majesty that commanded respect and awe rather than fear.

Though right now no one was displaying any interest in the thrones or any of the royal artefacts. Instead, her family were too busy talking, laughing and chatting and she allowed herself a moment to watch, to imprint this precious moment into memory.

Her parents were seated at the table, her mother holding her granddaughter on her lap, facing her, and Marisa gave a sudden smile—who would have thought Queen Kaamini would be so dotingly fond of a girl? But she was. And who could blame her? As Marisa looked at her daughter, who she and Kieran had named Amara Molly, after both their grandmothers, her heart turned over with sheer love.

A love she knew Kieran shared; he adored their daughter, loved spending time with her, and Amara already worshipped her father. Marisa looked over to her husband now as he spoke to his parents, who had come over for the ceremony. John and Becky Hamilton had proved to be wonderful parents-in-law and grandparents—Amara already had them wrapped round her little finger and Marisa knew any minute now Becky would claim a cuddle. If she could persuade the Queen to give Amara up.

Marisa smiled again as she saw Becky say something to Kieran, who grinned back as John laughed. She loved to see the easy interaction between the three of them, the way they included Marisa in that. She thought of the evenings spent playing cards and board games, thought too of all the childhood memories Becky had shared with her about Kieran, and the way her mother-in-law had hugged her after their first meeting. Hugged her and thanked her for bringing true happiness to her son.

Her gaze flitted now to Amit and Jai, both

asked to this gathering as close friends and people who felt like part of her family. She saw the two of them exchange a glance that held a certain something and she wondered if perhaps there was romance in the air, reminded herself to ask Rohan if Amit had said anything to him.

Marisa's gaze rested now on her brother and his wife. She recalled the beautiful private wedding ceremony of eight months before, where she had been the one to place the seven stones by the sacred fire and she and Kieran had watched hand in hand as Rohan and Elora exchanged their vows. And now she saw Elora look up at Rohan, saw her place her hand on her tummy in a gesture Marisa recognised and a sudden thrill of hope jolted through her. Her brother looked up and caught her eye and Marisa raised her eyebrows in the slightest of discreet questions. Rohan nudged Elora, who looked across to Marisa and gave the smallest of nods and a smile that spoke of her joy.

Marisa blinked back a sudden tear; she knew how much this meant to Elora and to Rohan, was glad too that Amara would soon have a cousin, and in the future hopefully a brother or sister.

And now Kieran was headed towards her and, as always, her heart did a hop, skip and a jump as he approached, handed her a small glass of champagne. 'Hello, beautiful wife, and newly crowned heir to Sarala.' His voice was low, his smile just for her, a smile that sent warmth and a small shiver over her skin. 'You were incredible today and you deserved every moment of that ceremony.' He took her hand in his.

'Thank you. For saying that and for being there over this last year. I couldn't have done it without you.' Because he'd supported, helped and been there, every step of the way. Somehow managed to juggle that with freelancing for Mix it Up.

He shook his head. 'This was all about you; you've worked so hard and Sarala is lucky to have you. And I'm lucky to have you. I love you, Marisa, and I always will.'

'As I do you.' And she knew they spoke the truth, that their marriage would go from strength to strength, based on a foundation of true love.

* * * * *

*If you missed the previous story in
the Royal Sarala Weddings duet,
then check out*
His Princess on Paper

*And if you enjoyed this story,
check out these other great reads
from Nina Milne*

Snowbound Reunion in Japan
Wedding Planner's Deal with the CEO
Consequence of Their Dubai Night

All available now!